Walter Parke

Lays of the Saintly

The new golden legend - with twelve page illustrations and vignette

Walter Parke

Lays of the Saintly
The new golden legend - with twelve page illustrations and vignette

ISBN/EAN: 9783337391393

Printed in Europe, USA, Canada, Australia, Japan

Cover: Foto ©Andreas Hilbeck / pixelio.de

More available books at **www.hansebooks.com**

𝕷𝖆𝖞𝖘 𝖔𝖋 𝖙𝖍𝖊 𝕾𝖆𝖎𝖓𝖙𝖑𝖞;

· OR,

THE NEW GOLDEN LEGEND.

By WALTER PARKE,

(THE LONDON HERMIT),

AUTHOR OF "SONGS OF SINGULARITY," "PEEPS AT LIFE," ETC.; JOINT-AUTHOR OF
"MANTEAUX NOIRS": A COMIC OPERA.

WITH TWELVE PAGE ILLUSTRATIONS AND VIGNETTE
By JOHN LEITCH.

London:
VIZETELLY & CO., 42 Catherine Street, Strand, W.C
E.V.
CB

Preface.

A BOOK of this kind, however harmless in its purpose, may yet be judged by some people to need a few words of apology. Despite the wide toleration of the present day, there are still persons who take exception to the humorous treatment of any subject even remotely connected with religion; and others who see in every jocose allusion to Saints and Miracles a studied irreverence towards the Roman Catholic form of Christianity.

No such offence, however, is herein intended; the object of raillery being, not any existing religion, but merely the superstition of the Middle Ages. Even this has only called forth a sort of good-natured ridicule, much in the same way as the Nursery Stories of our childhood, which may still afford entertainment, although we have long ceased to believe in them, or regard them with serious interest. The Saints of old were doubtless most meritorious personages, who did their best according to their lights, but their lights were not *our* lights, and the stronger illumination of nineteenth-century knowledge has cast them and their miraculous doings into the cold shade of myth and fable. Even their boasted virtues have become obsolete, and modern ideas of duty are very much at variance with those they entertained. To wear an iron belt night and day, to go without food for six weeks, to stand upon a pillar for twenty years, are not now-a-days the most accepted methods of getting to Heaven. But the records of the worthies who are credited with these extravagant feats of pious fervour have come down to us in such an exaggerated and distorted form that, while we may preserve some sympathy and respect for the Saints themselves, we can have none for their unveracious or over-credulous biographers.

Another objection may be that the Author has trespassed on the preserves of the immortal "Thomas Ingoldsby." If so, the offence is a trespass only, unattended with any illegal appropriation of property; the inimitable Barham has been already too much imitated, both as to matter and manner, and in the present "Lays" care has been taken to reduce this form of flattery to a minimum, by avoiding the style and metre most characteristic of that unique lyrist.

Less apology is needed for parodying standard poets. Travestie has long been a permitted form of pleasantry, and it can be indulged in without any disrespect to the originals. Not alone the mighty Masters of the Past, but such modern bards as Tennyson, Longfellow, Browning, and Swinburne, stand upon too lofty pedestals for them to be injured by any satiric shafts our toy-bow may let fly in their direction.

The writer, however, in justice to himself, should not be too hasty to class this and similar effusions as mere "trifles." Such they are, no doubt, in point of literary value; such they may appear to the practised critic who "polishes them off," a dozen at a time; and to the nimble reader who skips from page to page with all the agility of a mountain-goat; but the author who has learnt by experience that easy reading is not necessarily easy writing, is naturally unwilling to have his work thus lightly regarded. There has always been a vague idea that humorous verse is something especially easy to manufacture—something that can be "dashed off" at idle moments, almost without an effort. This may be the case with a few specially-gifted geniuses; but many years' constant practice in what is commonly called "comic writing" (although it is in reality among the gravest of mental occupations), has failed to give the present writer that enviable facility, and he is much disposed to believe (paradoxical as it may seem) that it is the novice who "dashes off" and the adept who finds it necessary to take pains.

The "Lays" were originally published several years ago in the *Dublin University Magazine*, the subject being suggested to the Author by the late Durham Dunlop, M.R.I.A., at that time its Editor and Proprietor.

THE HERMITAGE, LONDON, W.C.
    Nov. 20th, 1882.

CONTENTS.

ILLUSTRATIONS.

TO

MONTAGUE VIZETELLY,

IN RECOGNITION OF OUR LONG FRIENDSHIP,

AND OF MUCH GOOD COUNSEL

AND ENCOURAGEMENT

IN THIS AND OTHER LITERARY EFFORTS,

THIS BOOK

is cordially dedicated.

Prelude to the Lays.

 YE who love o'er dusty tomes to pore,
    To hear strange tales, and stories quaint and
      olden,
  List to some marvels that were told of yore
    In that black-letter Legend called the Golden,
Whence Butler's " Lives of Saints "—immortal works—
  Full of that piety called superstition
By certain readers (unbelieving Turks !)
  Who take the "anti-miracle " position.
To briefer lays these lengthy yarns I'll squeeze,
  Like floods of wine distilled into a chalice,
And, whomsoe'er I may offend or please,
  " Extenuate nought, and set down nought in malice."

LAYS OF THE SAINTLY.

No. I.—ST. SIMEON STYLITES.

I.

F all the ornaments to Christianity
    Who shone like stars upon the saintly roll,
    By treating earthly joys as sin and vanity,
    Spiting the body to preserve the soul ;
Of all these mortifiers of the flesh,
    Most glorious as a human-nature-killer,
With fame that time can only make more fresh
    ST. SIMEON stands—he stands upon a pillar.

II.

Son of a shepherd on the Syrian border,
    He had celestial visions when a boy ;
At twelve he join'd some strict monastic order,
    And thence self-torment seem'd his chiefest joy ;
He took to fasting six days in the week,
    And would the seventh, but he was prevented,

A

He made himself the humblest of the meek,
    But still this devotee was not contented :
In holy works yet more he would excel,
    A higher pitch of sanctity arrive at,
And so he took a rope from out a well,
    And round his body twisted it in private.

III.

So close the saint his penal girdle drew,
    He nearly died a victim to tight-lacing ;
The abbey surgeon had enough to do,
    The torturous cincture with his knife displacing.
Would this suffice? Oh, no ! the monk's devotion
    To greater lengths and deeper channels went ;
Anon he deem'd 'twould be a splendid notion
    To fast throughout the forty days of Lent.
So to a hermitage he next retired,
    Good Abbot Bassus left him bread and cup,
And coming to him when the time expired,
    Found that he'd taken neither bite nor sup !
Most persons would have died of sheer starvation,
    No "fasting girl" could go without so long ;
Yet Simeon lived, altho' in great prostration.
    (O! for a constitution half as strong !)

IV.

But, like the Corsair chief described by Byron,
    " His mind seem'd nourish'd by that abstinence,"

And tho' with woes his life he did environ,
  The spiritual profit was immense.
"Practice makes perfect," and a fortnight's fast
  Into six weeks may afterwards be stretchèd.
And Simeon found, as thus his Lents he pass'd,
  The holy happiness of being wretched.
At first, 'tis said, he stood upright to pray,
  Himself of rest as well as food denying,
Anon he sat, till, Nature giving way,
  He pray'd—like Pharisaic people—*lying.*

V.

Mortification, and the stern desire
  To quell desire, and stifle human feeling
Grow with their growth, the zealot did aspire
  To further processes of soul-annealing ;
So, on a mountain near to Antioch,
  In solitary torture next we find him,
Chain'd up by heavy fetters to a rock,
  Till told that *Will* should be enough to bind him ;
And then he hit upon a novel mode
  Of self-excruciation—'twas no less
Than taking up his permanent abode
  Upon a pillar in the wilderness.
How strange to think, by voluntary loss
  Of ev'ry human joy, to serve his Maker !
And, to gain Heav'n, become a sort of cross
  Between Prometheus and a Hindoo fakir !

VI.

Just think of what the holy man went through ;
 Fancy existing on the stony summit
Of a high column, where the wild winds blew,
 And overhead, with nought to overcome it,
No shelter or protection from its rays,
 The fierce and burning Oriental sun,
And there to linger out the weary days
 With frequent fast, and penance ever done !
~~And~~ animated Duke of York, or Nelson,
 A Wellington upon a narrow arch,
Clad in a cloak of skins, with nothing *else* on,
 Tho' rain may drench, or tropic heat may parch.

VII.

To make a trial of the saint's humility,
 The bishops sent him orders to descend
And close his penance, so, with all facility,
 The martyr 'gan to this command attend ;
But ere he could step off his sacred perch,
 Again to join the world he had forsaken,
The much-admiring fathers of the Church
 Sent word that downward' step need not be taken.
His heart, I can't help thinking, *must* have felt
 A shade of disappointment overspread it
To see so fine a chance for ever melt
 Of quitting such a martyrdom with credit.

VIII.

Four years upon a pillar nine feet high,
  Three on another, rising just eighteen,
Ten on a third, still nearer to the sky,
  The various seasons had St. Simeon seen ;
And on the last, when death put in his claim,
  A score of years—in total, thirty-seven !
After all this—it *would* have been a shame .
  Had our Stylites fail'd to get to Heaven :
You see he mounted thither by degrees,
  Ascending as his high ambition vaulted,
Yet prideful thoughts he scatter'd to the breeze,
  Humbling himself the more he was exalted.

IX.

Such was his life ; 'twas pray'r, and pray'r, and pray'r,
  One long unwearied round of rapt devotion,
So oft repeated his prostrations were
  He nearly had attained Perpetual Motion.
One pilgrim had the hardihood to count
  The times the saint with bowing did adore,
And when 'twas added up, the whole amount
  O'ertopped twelve hundred by just forty-four !
That is, for every minute and a half
  Twice did the martyr bend his spinal column,
For sixteen hours a day—'twould make us laugh,
  But that the subject is so very solemn.

X.

Oh ! our degenerate days !—a modern saint
  (If saints there were) at such an exercise
Ere noon-day would become so weak and faint,
  He fain must rest him till the morrow's rise ;
And even then, a week or so would kill him :
  But saints of old were made of stouter stuff,
And heav'nly strength did so sustain and fill him,
  Years pass'd yet Simeon cried not " Hold, enough ! "

XI.

Yet not supreme was his superiority
  To human weakness, flesh at last must fail ;
The Golden Legend, on the best authority,
  Gives all his sufferings in close detail ;
How loathsome sores his tortured limbs afflicted,
  And foul disease within his members sat,
Till to *one leg* his standing was restricted,
  And, *for a year or more*, he stood on that !
How many a horrid, noisome, living thing
  Beset him, and how one of these, out-hopping
In presence of a certain Paynim king,
  To whom the saint was words of wisdom dropping —
Pick'd up by him, became a gem of price,
  A gratifying change, and wondrous token ;
But such particulars are far from nice,
  And modern bards must not be *too* outspoken.

XII.

Talking of bards, one day a pagan poet
Approach'd the pillar, and began to sing ;
The blessed Simeon could not choose but know it,
  So high the minstrel pitch'd his voice and string.
This bard was Greek in sentiment and style ;
  A Venus-worshipper—profuse of curses
On those who deem'd his ethics loose and vile :
  I give you a translation of his verses :—

STYLITES.

" Closed eyelids that hide like a shutter,
  Hard eyes that have visions apart,|
The grisly gaunt limbs, and the utter
  And deadly abstraction of heart ;
Whence all that is joyous and bright is
  Expell'd as both vicious and vain,
O, stony and stolid Stylites,
  Our Patron of Pain !

" There can be but warfare between us,
  For thine is a spiritual creed,
And mine is the worship of Venus,
  On " raptures and roses " I feed ;
Self-torture's thine only employment,
  We both feel the bliss and the bane,
For woe will oft spring from enjoyment,   .
  Our Patron of Pain !

" Can joys be of Martyrdom's giving?
     Men seek them, and change at a breath
The leisures and labours of living,
     For the ravings and rackings of death :
To stand all alone on that height is
     An action unsought and insane,
O, moveless and morbid Stylites,
     Our Patron of Pain !

" There are those who still offer to Bacchus,
     There are men who Love's goddess still own,
What right have new faiths to attack us ?
     And why are our shrines overthrown ?
There are poets, inspired by Castalia,
     Whose lyres have Anacreon's strain,
Whose lives are one long saturnalia,
     Our Patron of Pain !

" We sing of voluptuous blisses,
     Of all that thy rigour would spurn,
Of "biting " and "ravenous " kisses,
     Of bosoms that beat and that burn ;
To all that is earthy and carnal,
     Our votaries' souls we would chain,
We breathe of the chamber and charnel,
     Our Patron of Pain!

" Oho ! for the days of sweet vices,
     The glory of goddess and Greek !
(For all that most naughty and nice is
     Most purely and surely antique).

O ho ! for the days when Endymion
　　Thro' love o'er Diana did reign !
These, these were Elysian, St. Simeon,
　　Our Patron of Pain !

" We'll crown us with myrtle and laurel,
　　We'll wreathe us in Paphian flowers,
To be and make others immoral,
　　We'll ply our poetical powers ;
Our worship shall be Aphrodite's,
　　To woman the wine we will drain,
O, loveless and lonely Stylites,
　　Our Patron of Pain !

" By the hunger thine abstinence causes,
　　By the thirst of unbearable heat,
By thy pray'rs which have very few pauses,
　　By thy lodging devoid of a seat,
By sleep that so meagre at night is,
　　'Twere better awake to remain,
Come down from thy pillar, Stylites,
　　Our Patron of Pain ! "

XIII.

The holy man, it need not be remark'd,
　　Turn'd as deaf ear to such lascivious singing
As when a serpent hiss'd, or wild dog bark'd,
　　Or raven croak'd around his column winging ;

Immovable in body as in mind,
  He bore his life's insufferable tedium,
It seems a pity that he could not find
  'Twixt vice and virtue's height some " happy medium."

XIV.

So guarded was the saint against exposure
  To e'en the shadow of a shade of sin,
No female foot might tread that blest inclosure,
  Even his mother could not enter in ;
She came to see him after many years,
  But hallow'd barriers kept them still asunder,
Maternal grief outpour'd in bitter tears,
  Three days, three nights, and then she died (no wonder!).

XV.

In pause of pray'r, the saint would shed his blessing
  On those who flock'd from each adjacent town,
The throng in pious homilies addressing,
  But as his sermons were not taken down,
We know not of the nature of his teaching ;
  He *stood so high*, they could not but revere him ;
And if he *had* a fault, it was in preaching
  Over the heads of those who came to hear him.
Folks used his image as a charm, in Rome ;
  Kings, queens, and princes sought his benediction,
Both lay and cleric for advice would come :
  He gave to all who ask'd, without restriction.

XVI.

Goodness on earth, if carried to extremes,
　Will gift a man with superhuman powers
(At least 'twas thus in olden times, it seems,
　Tho' not so in this sceptic age of ours) ;
A saint was nothing in those saintly days,
　Unless he bade to Nature's laws defiance,
And acted in a thousand startling ways,
　Quite unexplainable by modern science.
Simeon wrought miracles, like other saints,
　By pray'r he made the desert bring forth water ;
By touch he cured most dangerous complaints ;
　By sacred charms a leopard he did slaughter.

XVII.

Here is a miracle, as strange as true :
　A dreaded dragon dwelt in that direction,
So venomous, no vegetation grew
　Around its cave ; whose breath was rank infection.
This monster ran a stake into its eye
　(How the mischance befell, we are not told),
It crawled into the monastery nigh,
　And their its piteous tail it did unfold;
And blind and bleeding, moan'd in doleful case,
　But no one help'd it—all were too afraid ;
And harmless lay three days outside the place,
　And then resolved to seek St. Simeon's aid.
Thus did the dragon, to the column'd pile,
　Drag on its dragonistic length of frame,
And tell—we know not in what tongue or style—
　Its occupant the reason why it came.

The saint was touch'd, "Anoint the injured feature
  With mud," he said, and pray'd with all his strength ;
They did, and from the optic of the creature,
  Pull'd out a spike of eighteen inches' length !

XVIII.

One marvel more : a woman rashly drinking,
  Swallow'd by accident a little snake,
Hid in the cup, the reptile doubtless thinking
  That it or she had made some grand mistake.
For years this living incubus possess'd her,
  She tried all remedies, but quite in vain,
And all the while, the burden that oppress'd her,
  Each year increased its size, its victim's pain ;
At last she sought the saint, in him confiding,
  Implored his aid in righting what was wrong,
Her lips he did anoint, and out came sliding·
  A monstrous serpent of three cubits long !
Some critics stigmatize as mere inventions
  These deeds which possibilities forbid,
And say that serpents of such large dimensions,
  They cannot swallow, if the woman did.

XIX.

But e'en the miracles in life he wrought
  Were less than those accruing from his death,
As if the very atmosphere had caught
  Some Magic power from his parting breath ;

The odour from his body was a strong
   And sweet perfume—a fact most unexpected
And wonderful, considering how long
   All laws of wholesomeness he had neglected.
Birds, beasts, and men (and fishes too, no doubt)
   So loudly wail'd to learn the saint was dead.
Their cries were heard seven miles, or thereabout,
   Hills, fields, grew sad ; a black cloud loom'd o'erhead,
Wherein a seraph clothed in light appear'd,
   With other visions equally angelic.
The Pope of Antioch, who seized the beard
   Of Simeon's corpse to keep it as a relic,
Felt his hand wither'd, pulseless, stiff, and numb ;
   A dozen pray'rs were needful to restore it ;
The body cured a man both deaf and dumb,
   As to its latest resting-place they bore it.

XX.

Like all great men, St. Simeon set a fashion
   (Carried by monks and masons to great height)
And pillar-martyrdom was still a passion,
   Tho' quench'd was his celestial beacon light,
His followers were " Stylites," " Pillarists,"
   " Air-martyrs," " Pillar-saints," and " Holy birds."
They flourish'd long, but now no trace exists
   Of all they did and suffer'd, save the words
Written in monkish hist'ry's glowing page ;
   But Simeon's name stands prominent and single,
And e'en in this unsympathetic age,
   His story well befits the poet's jingle.

So runs St. Simeon's tale ; if aught too large
   Therein appears for modern faith to swallow,
Dear reader, pray don't lay it to the charge
   Of one who humbly seeks the truth to follow ;
Think, rather, that in long-revolving time,
   Transcribers, vivid in imagination,
To make their lofty theme still more sublime,
   May have infused some *slight* exaggeration ;
Ev'n Alban Butler, with a charming candour,
   And simple faith in what he has to state,
Owns that Stylites' pious deeds were grander
   That moderns should attempt to imitate ;
This age would judge that, if indeed he bore
   One tithe the horrors that they say beset him,
His madness we must pity and deplore,
   And blame the cruelty of those that let him.
At least our moral no one can mistake—
   'Tis that, to make secure our future bliss,
To gain the better world, *we ought to make*
   Ourselves as wretched as we can in this !

No. 2.—ST. MACARIUS.

THE Saints on our list will be many and various,
   And drawn from all quarters, abroad and at
   home :
      The one we now take is the hermit Macarius,
Who's held in particular honour at Rome
Three weeks ere the sun enters into Aquarius,
   And reigns for the day in each cloister and dome.

The " Mac " may seem Irish, or else Caledonian,
   But names are not always a question of race
(Thus " George Psalmanazar" was no Babylonian),
   And old Alexandria in Egypt's the place
Where erst our Macarius lived as confectioner,
   And dwelt in the manifold *sweets* of this life,
Till, seeing how folks did in ev'ry direction err,
   And how Man and Virtue are always at strife,
He sigh'd, " I am sick of the world and its pleasures,
   I'll hie to the desert, and dwell in a cave,
And while I am hoarding up heavenly treasures,
   I'll live on the money I've managed to save."

For then it was common for clerical shepherds
   To weary of all men—including their flocks,
And dwell far away, like the lions and leopards,
   In depths of the forests or holes in the rocks.

A custom, once started, will spread very quickly,
    Example's a tree most prolific of fruit ;
Soon Egypt with eremites' cells was so thickly
    Besprinkled, their number was hard to compute.
The monks, who subsisted by bodily labour,
    With pray'rs very many, and wants very few,
Were ready to welcome our Saint as a neighbour,
    When he from society's evils withdrew ;
So courteous were they to each neophyte brother,
    That one of these wearers of sandals and gowns
Would leave him his hut, and move on to another ;
    Oh ! where will you meet with such kindness in towns ?

For sixty long years the recluse did continue
    A life of such rigour, and hardship, and toil,
That, tann'd in complexion, and harden'd in sinew,
    His aspect was rugged and dry as the soil.
On pulse and raw herbs—(what a splendid digestion
    Is shown by the fact !)—seven years did he live ;
All animal viands seem'd out of the question,
    Tho' lower in price than we *now* have to give.
Three following years upon bread he subsisted,
    And that only four or five ounces a day,
In Lent 'twas astonishing how he existed,
    So little he took till that Fast pass'd away.

Tho' not a Stylites in mortification,
    Macarius oft did the body afflict,
For fear that the course of devout meditation
    Might haply be troubled by subjects less strict :

ST. MACARIUS'S ENTOMOLOGICAL MARTYRDOM.

One day in his cell, 'tis asserted by Butler,
  The anchorite chanced to be stung by a gnat;
No torture on earth could be sharper or subtler.
  Cried he, " A good hint ! I must act upon that ;
In Scete's wide marshes the wild flies are swarming,
  Whose stings even pierce thro' the hide of a boar—
This body I'll yield to their fighting and storming,
  To drive out the sins that afflict me so sore."

He went, and the insects attack'd him like savages,
  And caused an *inferno* of exquisite pain ;
Six months he remain'd there, exposed to their ravages,
  Then thought it high time to wend homeward again.
From head to foot cover'd with blister and swelling,
  The saint out of all recognition had grown,
So fearful his aspect—so strange and repelling,
  That only by *voice* could he make himself known !
Ev'n *that*, one would think, must have roughen'd to coarse-
      ness,
  And sounded untunefully frog-like and harsh,
At least, people now-a-days suffer from hoarseness,
  Tho.' far less exposed than the monk in the marsh.

The names of the saintly are so multifarious,
  To keep them distinct oft surpasses our pow'rs.
And forty miles off lived another Macarius—
  " The Elder "—pray do not confound him with ours,
For *he* was " the Younger "—what aids the confusion
  Their dates in the calendar run very near ;
And in the Greek Church they adopt the inclusion
  Of both of their feasts on *one* day of the year.

B

These devotee name-sakes were sometimes together
    Seen gravely hob-nobbing their monachal cowls,
But seldom ; for hermits, tho' birds of a feather,
    Dwell most in *complete* isolation—like owls.

In ages of yore, as you know, my dear readers,
    Those demons, whose names now offend " ears polite,"
To gobble up souls,like omnivorous feeders,
    Walk'd boldly about, plain and ugly to sight ;
Macarius oft by such fiends was accosted,
    But fearless and staunch, he upheld the good cause,
And many a wretch who would else have been roasted,
    Was rescued by him from the enemy's claws.
Once Lucifer came, with a scythe on his shoulder,
    To slay the good father, but could not prevail,
In danger Macarius only grew bolder,
    And, when well resisted, the Devil turns tail.

The saint once had taken—(the act seems peculiar)
    The corpse of a pagan to pillow his head,
Some fiends passing by growl'd, "This clerical *fool* here
    Is playing a game with our forfeited dead.
Wake, sinner ! and yield ye to those you belong to."
    " I can't," said the corpse, " for the saint holds me tight."
"He shan't!" cried the saint, for you'll find me too strong to
    Give way, tho' you pull him with main and with might.
Get up, if you will " (he address'd the deceased one),
    And gave him a blow with his sanctified fist,
The demons all fled, from the chief to the least one,
    They saw that 'twere idle such force to resist.

That fiend, whose appropriate title's *Abaddon*,
   Who's blacker by nature than mortals can paint
And crafty as villains by Collins or Braddon,
   However, at times, stole a march on our saint.
The latter set out o'er the desert to travel,
   A plain without finger-post footpath, or stile,
In order, returning, his way to unravel
   He planted a rod at the end of each mile ;
But Satan, so watchful as well as malicious,
   Pull'd up every stick that he found on the track,
Said he, as he laughed at an act so flagitious,
   "'Twill puzzle old-Macky to find his way back ! "
The reeds in a bundle were tied by the demon,
   And found by the saint when he woke from his sleep,
He felt all abroad, like a compassless seaman,
   Yet back to his latitude managed to creep.

The elder and younger Macarius to*get*her in
   A skiff o'er the breast of old Nilus did float—
How touching (and rare) to see clerical brethren
   In sweet unanimity *row in one boat !*
A tribune, remarking they looked so contented,
   Was struck by the bliss such a life could secure,
Of all of his sins in a lump he repented,
   Went home, sold his goods, and gave all to the poor,
And took to the Cœnobite life, like Macarius,
   Ah ! would *we* had saints who could lead or persuade
An age that's so frivolous, worldly, gregarious,
   To feel the delights of seclusion's calm shade !

'Tis true, some have tried it without satisfaction ;
    One own'd that the world he preferred, on the whole,
And thought a good life of example and action
    Might benefit man, and advantage the soul ;
But holy Macarius saw how distorted
    By Satan's insidious wiles was the mind
That thus could be sway'd, so he warmly exhorted
    The monk not to think of rejoining mankind.

One day on the road, where some robber had slain him,
    Or beasts of the desert his life had despatch'd,
Macarius picked up the head of a Paynim,
    Without any sign of a body attach'd.
The skull of a Yorick—for Hamlet has proved it—
    If properly handled, a lesson may teach, ˎ
This head, when the sage to his table removed it,
    Did more, for it exercised reason and speech !

" O, where is the soul that thy body once harbour'd ? "
    Ask'd the saint, and the head would have pointed below,
But having no fingers, turned larboard and starboard,
    In mournfullest shake, and then answer'd, " *You* know."

" Is the place very deep ? " said the reverend querist,
    " More deep," said the head, "than from heaven to earth."
" And pray doth *thy* soul to the bottom lie nearest ? "
    " No ; many a one has a far lower berth,
The *Jews* are much further from pardon and glory
    Than *my* wretched *manes*, and suffer more pain."
(O, think of *this*, Rothschild and Montefiore !
    Whatever your merits, you'll find them in vain).

The saint's curiosity still was untiring,
  " If Israelite souls are so low as you say,
Can any sink lower ?—'tis worth the inquiring."
  " Oh, yes ! the *false Christians*, a very long way ! "
Such evidence, passing man's power of giving,
  Was precious as gold to the saint who could win it,
Thought he, " Tho' some numbskulls we find 'mid the living,
  This head of the dead has at last *something* IN IT."

More wonders besides in the life are recorded
  Of this most respected and excellent man,
The noble example his deeds have afforded
  We all ought to follow—*as far as we can;*
The span of his pious career was extended
  Till nature, exhausted, could hold out no more,
So, blest and lamented, his pilgrimage ended,
  He died—Anno Domini, three-ninety-four.

So often the Saint o'er the Devil was victor,
  So valiantly faced he Apollyon's spear,
To rescue poor souls from the torture-inflictor,
  He ought to be known as " The Saint without fear,"
The patron of all who are brave to audacity,
  High-spirited, recklessly bold and hilarious ;
And thus, to describe him with force and veracity,
  We aptly might call him " St. *Devil-may-care*-ius."

No. 3.—MORTE D'EDMUND:

AN IDYLL OF THE KING.

I waited for the 'bus at Oxford Street,
I stood with touts and shoeblacks on the herb,
I watch'd the passing throng, and then I shaped
An ancient Saxon legend into this :—

EDMUND the Good, Edmund the Wonderful,
Edmund the Saintly King of Angle-land,
High in the regal halls of Hagelsdune,
Sat girt with knights ; his many-muscled form
Clothed in fine flannel, 'lastic, comf'table,
Enrich'd with oroide, and Bristol gems
Of pastiest sheenery ; his brow sustain'd
The aluminium coronal of power.
Closed were his optics, and his kingly nose
Tip-tilted like the handle of a jug,
And his long locks of auricomous gold
Were such as might have deck'd Sir Lancelot,
Sir Bevidere, or Galahad the good,
Or HIM who held the Great Pendragonship,
And ate his dinner off the Table Round.

That afternoon a Summer-dreaminess
Reign'd in the regal halls of Hagelsdune,
The sunlight jigg'd upon the plaster'd wall,
And nodding pear-trees bobb'd against the panes,

The blue-fly humm'd a tune, the while, without,
The murmur of innumerous spelling-bees
Fell on the ear, and mingling came the roll
Of skates from where, athwart an inner room,
Wheel-footed, many maidens of the court
In airy fairy lightness skimm'd the floor ;
So blent the lulling sounds, and all was peace.

Sudden the silence into pieces smash'd,
With tumult that to bursting fill'd the place ;
And swarming in the halls of Hagelsdune,
A tribe of Pagan Danes, all arm'd and mail'd,
And thirsting equally for blood and beer,
Led by a bulky bandit, with a head
Like densest door-mat, startled all the Court,
No greeting gave, but made themselves at home,
And all unbidden grabb'd the food and wine,
While gruff their leader faced the Saintly King.

"Thus saith my Chieftain, Hinguar the Dane,
Victor of many tribes upon these shores :
' Tell Edmund he must share his kingdom with me,
Own me his suzerain, and to me resign
One-half his treasures, whether gems or gold,
Silver, mosaic, or electro-plate,
On pain of fate too terrible to name ;
Tell him my will is law, and that unless
He give me half, no quarter shall he have.' "

Then Edmund held a parley with his knights,
And ask'd his bishops what he'd better do ;
So, like a dozen in a jury box,
They wrangled for an hour, till, all agreed,
The king turned envoy-wards, and thus replied :—

" I will not share my kingdom with the Dane,
I will not swear allegiance to his might,
I will not halve my wealth with Hinguar ;
Tell him he needs rise early in the morn
To get the slightest boon or gain from me ;
Tell him to go to Jericho or Bath ;
This tell him, with King Edmund's compliments."

Back spurr'd the rugged Norseman to his chief,
And found him arm'd in proof, sharpening his sword,
And quaffing hugeous draughts of Danish ale ;
Fierce as a creature born of *Lyonesse*,
Or wild inhabitant of *Tiger* Bay,
Eager to slaughter all who cross'd his will ;
And brief the soldier told him all in all—
How Saxon Edmund had defied his power.

Then strode the fierce Dane up and down the hall,
And took his carrot locks between his teeth,
And could not speak for swearing ; whilst his eyes
Flash'd fire that might have set the place in flames,
And crozzled up the furniture to dust ;
Choked had he been with rage and Northern oaths
But that the flowing flagon wash'd them down.

"Am I to be defied ?   By Odin, Thor,
Freyga and Seatur, Sun and Moon and Tuisco,
This must not be !   Have out ten thousand spears,
Saddle my steed, and we will issue forth
And slaughter all the Saxons we can find ;
Edmund I'll kill more dead than all the rest,
And of his churls my sword Excrucior
Shall chop and fritter twenty million lives ! "

Thunder'd the Pagan's charger thro' the wold,
Crushing the snails beneath his iron hoofs,
Making each leaf, like aspens, quake with fear ;
The birds were scared from song ; the timid bull
Trembled and fled ; the bold-faced rabbit " cut "
Before the wrathful gaze of Hinguar.

And soon the horrid din of clashful fight
Disturbed the tasteful grounds of Hagelsdune,
And play'd Old Harry with the garden-beds.
The Saxon band, led by the sainted king,
Fought man to man, or rather man to men :
For them outnumb'ring far, the Danish force
Bore down upon them like a thousand bricks ;
The air with arrows was as dark as night,
Tho' shone the sun in that tremendous shine ;
And in the midmost charging, Hinguar
Drove his long spear thro' many men at once
 A feat well-worthy of Sir *Lance-a-lot*),
Or with his Viking axe or Runic mace
Knock'd down some three or four at ev'ry blow ;

And ev'n the stoutest knight, whose twenty stone
Might make the dwindled "Claimant" smite the beam,
Went down before him, as the fluent pap
Goes down the throat of meek-eyed infancy.
Borne on a piebald-horse, whose kick was death,
Crash'd on the Dane, the leaders each to each
Oft urged, for in the thick St. Edmund rode.
Clothed in fine flannel, 'lastic, comf'table,
But over that a coat of ringéd mail
(Head helm-crowned), and pitch'd into Hinguar
As "virtuous peasant" on transpontine boards
Struggles with "'ardened ruffian"—so the King.

And all day long the noise of battle roll'd,
Till earth and heaven were hush'd to hear its din ;
The very thunder own'd itself outvoiced,
And sunk to silence, broken by a roar
Which shook the air a thousand miles around.
The hardy Breton, trembling, heard the row,
In German forests, and on Scottish hills,
O'er Norway's fjords, and Schleswig-Holstein's downs,
Thro' bogg'd Hibernia, and leek-teeming Wales,
The echos lingered—ending when they ceased ;
Until the Saxon knights could brook no more
The Danish numerosity of men.
'Twas twelve to one—long odds against the good ;
And heaps lay slain, heaps more had run away,
And other heaps fell captive, till alone
King Edmund still fought on, with ring by ring
Hack'd off his hauberk, all his weapons broke,

ST. EDMUND'S LAST FIGHT.—A MEDIÆVAL "SIX HUNDRED."

And not an inch of skin without a wound,
So judged it time to yield him to the foe,
Who, when they clapp'd the rusty darbies on,
Laugh'd like hyænas.—And so closed the fight.

And while the sun still linger'd in the east,
Where in those ages it was wont to set,
And cast his golden beams across the lawns,
And deck'd the ditches, green with water-cress,
The savage Danes led out the blameless King,
Clothed in fine flannel, 'lastic, comf'table,
Fearful of nought but fear, and dreading dread,
And cowardly of showing cowardice,
That was the sort of man King Edmund was.
So rode they till they stopp'd ; a poplar there
Flung wide its sturdy arms athwart the mere,
To this they tied him, and began to flog
With rods that long in pickle had been steep'd,
With birch, the same that grocers put in tea,
With leather straps of toughest donkey hide.
He bore it like a lamb, whereat enraged,
Cried Hinguar, " Let's make a butt of him,
For ridicule to kings is worse than pain,
Shoot ! " so their arrows sought the living mark
Unmissingly, till he was riddled so
'Twas quite a riddle how he lived so long,
But still the regal martyr would not die.
At length the Dane, impatient, swore and growl'd,
" Excrucior shall end him," so he drew

His notchy brand from out its war-worn sheath,
Raised high the fateful blade, and with a sweep of it,
The auburn-tressed head roll'd on the sward ;
This Hinguar picking up, and yelling " Play ! "
As one who bowls when cricket is the game,
He hurl'd the missile far into a bush.

Meanwhile such doughty knights of Edmund's court
As with discretion—valour's better part—
Had fled the massacre, and safely hid
Within the vinous vaults of Hagelsdune,
Had heard the trample of the foe o'erhead,
Had heard the echoes striking on the walls,
And the long arrows whizz along the air,
Till by degrees the tumult died away,
And all was vanish'd, as the mountain dew,
Melts from the spirit-haunted Glenlivát.
Now, seeing all was clear, they issued forth
And found no foe, but found the headless king
Tied to the tree.   Some wept, some ran away,
But others took another corse (the king's),
But wonder'd where on earth his head had gone.

And so they sought and sought throughout the wold,
And calling to each other, " Where are *you ?* "
A voice like Edmund's answered, " Here ! here ! here "
As do the members of a ministry
When telling " points " adorn their leader's speech.
Mazed at the marvel, follow'd swift the knights,

And came where lay the head, and, strange to say,
A grey gaunt wolf was guarding it, and wept
The bitterest tears such creature ever shed,
Tamed to unwolfly gentleness by grief.
But let me tell the story in the words
Of one who, in a happier olden day,
Was Laureate in the halls of Hagelsdune.

    Home they brought the martyr dead,
      Many wept, the rest did cry,
    But they could not find his head,
      Much as ever they might try.

    Rose a page with chubby face,
      Softly to the scull'ry crept,
    Deeming *that* must be the place,
      Where the victims' heads were kept !

    Then they sought him high and low,
      Call'd him—lo ! the voice they loved
    Answering show'd them where the foe
      Had the kingly skull removed.

    Rose a wolf of sixty years,
      Paw'd the head beneath his knee,
    Murmuring, " Here it is, my dears,
      Do not be afraid of me ! "

This did they, and took up the sainted king.
Back to the regal halls of Hagelsdune
They bore him, follow'd by the weeping wolf.

Then with a loving care and brush of glue
They join'd the body neatly to the head,
The junction held, until a thin red rim
Alone remain'd to show the sever'd place.
St. Edmund's buried at St. Edmundsbury,
And o'er his tomb such miracles were wrought
As Maskelyne or Merlin far outdid :
The blind receivèd sight to look on him,
The deaf could fancy that they heard his voice,
The dumb could praise his virtues, and be heard,
The stingy loosed the strings of heart and purse,
And emptied coppers on his sacred shrine ;
When once some sacrilegious burglars came,
To filch, with fiendish felony of fist,
The gold and silver of his sepulchre,
A sudden seizure, strange, invisible,
Clutch'd them as tightly as galvanic shock,
And kept them fix'd all night, and when the dawn,
Show'r'd down its golden beams upon their guilt,
The men were found, were taken in the act,
Quickly " run in," and tried by righteous judge,
No option of a fine, but twenty years
Ticket-of-leave-less, served they out their time.

No. 4.—ST. CRISPIN AND ST. CRISPINIAN.

THE "Snobs," whom Thackeray so finely drew,
    Have brought that name to well-deserved con-
      tempt ;
From which the honest maker of a shoe,
   Slipper, or boot, should always be exempt ;
The latter kind alone the blessing share
Of being under sainted patrons' care.

Saints Crispin and Crispinian—for saints,
   Tho' single men, in fame are sometimes double—
Were born in Rome ; and no plebeian taints
   Dimm'd the "blue blood" that in their veins did bubble.
Yet took they to a course which shocks gentility—
Street preaching, sandal-making, and humility.

Like certain modern teachers near at hand,
   These worthy brothers noted less the crimes
That stalk'd so rampant thro' their native land
   Than others prevalent in farther climes ;
Perchance they deem'd the Romans past all saving,
   And long'd more hopeful regions to explore.
Perhaps to see the world they felt a craving ;
   At least they bade adieu to Tiber's shore,
Roam'd past the Alps, and lastly settled down

'Mid Celtic warriors and Teutonic carles,
At Soissons, afterwards the regal town
    Of Pepin, Clovis, Chilperic, and Charles,
There set to work to civilize the Frank,
To win men's souls, and break the devil's bank.

All day St. Crispin and his brother wrought
    At missionary work, and when the night
To other men repose from labour brought,
    They set to shoemaking with all their might ;
For saints can't live, chameleon-like, on air
    (Tho' some, we've seen, have tried it now and then).
And so they labour'd with a duplex care,
    Both day and night upon the *soles* of men.
A mystic silence doth the legend keep
On how they managed to dispense with sleep.

Some pagans were converted by the aid
    Of soundly evangelic eloquence ;
But more by reason that their saintships' trade
    Touched them thro' interest and outward sense—
Their worldly souls thus indirectly reaching.
    Mere argument to such will bear no fruits ;
And Crispin, in addition to his teaching,
    Gave each fresh convert a new pair of boots ;
To be a sign that, by his Christian vow,
He stood upon *another footing* now.

'Tis thus that, 'neath the burning sun of Ind,
  Where sober Mussulman and Hindoo bask ;
Our zealous missionaries often find
  Their pious labours but a barren task.
So little can their rhetoric prevail
  With men in error's ways so deeply sunk,
Except a few who, having tasted ale,
  Embrace the Cross in order to—get drunk !
How many " natives " to the fold have come
Lured less by Christianity than rum ?

So throve our saints amazingly, and drew
  The heathen Franks in thousands to their tether ;
Up to their time no mortal ever knew
  Such proselyting virtue dwelt in leather.
But native cobblers of the older creed,
  With indignation view'd the rival stall ;
And making piety a cloak for greed,
  Denounced them to the Cæsar, then in Gaul,
Maximian Herculius, who referr'd
The case to Rictius Varus to be heard.

A man whose hate of Christians never slept,
  Who fain would have " improved away " the race,
Rictius most gladly did the task accept.
  Soon stood the saints before his awful face ;
Such tyrants were not wont to spend much time
  Upon the mere formalities of trial ;
Their sentence was enough to prove the crime ;
  Vain was extenuation or denial ;
C

Varus resolved to stay the spread of error,
By measures that should strike the world with terror.

Such tortures then the Crispins underwent,
    My pen would hardly venture to reveal them ;
But that, as Heaven its kind assistance sent,
    The persons most affected *did not feel them !*
At first the holy men were scourged with flails,
    Yet were they neither injured nor afraid,
Boot-brads were driven 'neath their finger nails,
    When lo ! an angel hasten'd to their aid ;
The brads flew out, " return'd to plague the inventors,"
And punish'd, not the victims, but tormentors.

But Varus' heart was harden'd, so he gave
    The dreadful order, " mill-stones, there, for two !
Tie to their necks and fling them in the wave,
    And *then* see what their saintly powers can do ? "
To hear was to obey, the hallow'd twain,
    Like kittens doom'd to drowning from their birth,
Souse in the Aisne were flung, but rose again,
    And, while the mill-stones sunk in bed of earth,
Clomb up the other bank, and reached the path,
Far more refresh'd than damaged by their bath.

Seeing that water but improved the saints
    (Saints as a rule did not affect the fluid),
Rictius, who knew compassion's soft restraints
    No more than arch-Inquisitor or Druid

Order'd a vessel filled with molten lead,
  And into this the blessed ones were thrust.
Still, Salamander-like, they showed no dread
  (How strong the will is when the faith's robust !)
And while the holy cobblers fail'd to die,
A splash of metal blinded Varus' eye.

In fiery furnace fed and fill'd with oil,
  And pitch—the " boiling *pitch* " of Fahrenheit—
The saints were cast, to " shuffle off life's coil,"
  And thereto, be annihilated quite.
An angel saved them ere they could consume ;
  Whereat the blood of Rictius boil'd with ire,
And dizzy with his anger and the fume,
  He lost his hold and tumbled in the fire.
Where, being made of common sinful clay,
  Not fortified with sanctity at all,
He quickly perish'd, to the deep dismay
  Of those who saw, but could not stop his fall.
Fierce at his fate, they turned their vengeful claws
Upon the Christians, whom they deem'd its cause.

" Off with their heads ; " the savage cry arose,
  The saints were seized, and—climax unexpected !—
The power that hitherto had baulk'd their foes
  No more their lives from martyrdom protected ;
The axe was raised, they died like you or I.
  But marvels at their death commenced afresh,
For tho' allow'd on open plain to lie,
  Vulture nor wolf would touch their sacred flesh ;

Which, on that eve, two pious pilgrims found,
And forthwith bore to consecrated ground.

These monks were old and feeble, and the weight
   Of slaughter'd saints is of decided gravity,
And how to bear them caused some slight debate ;
   When Providence, with most unlook'd-for suavity,
Suspended gravitation's tyrant force,
   " Till," says the legend, "free in frame and limb,
Each bearer felt not that he bore a corse,
   But just as if ' *the corse were bearing him;* ' "
No skiff had they, but on the river's verge
   The same mysterious hand had moor'd a boat.
Without an oar, or helm, or sail to urge
   Its burden'd way, yet did it swiftly float
Above the waves as smoothly as a dream,
Although their course was dead against the stream.

Here ends our strictly true, yet wond'rous tale,
   St. Crispin, as the elder of the firm,
Became, and will remain, till time doth fail,
   The patron saint of all to whom the term
Of " Snob "—respectfully pronounced—applies.
   Some able preachers have been men of leather,
And, after Crispin, need we feel surprise
   Boots and religion often go together ?
Reader, invoke his name whene'er a pair
   You wear for the first time, and if they *hurt* you,
Think on the martyrdom our saints went through,
   All for the good of trade, and truth, and virtue.

Our moral is, " We all have some weak part ;
  With some it is the body, some the head,
Others the will, and some, alas ! the heart,
  With our good patrons 'twas the *neck* instead.
And thus, tho' fire and water fail'd to end them,
Beheading could at once to heaven sent them.

No. 5—ST. GENEVIÈVE.

 PARIS ! Paris ! when thy maskèd balls
    Fill with the young and gay, the fair and frail,
    To revel thro' the night in dazzling halls
Where virtue certainly doth not prevail ;
When thousands play-wards on the Sabbath flock,
    To see the last new " spicy " bouffe or ballet,
To drink in Hervé, Offenbach, Lecocq,
    And chuckle o'er each too suggestive sally :
When pert *cocottes*, supreme in gilded vice,
    Along the streets their tinsel splendours flaunt,
And all that's " naughty " is so far from " nice "
    As to obtrude in every public haunt,—
Who would suppose thou hast for patroness
    A virgin Saint of wondrous holy living ?
If she can know thee, yet protect and bless,
    Her nature must indeed be most forgiving !

I.

St. Geneviève was nurtured in Nanterre,
  In the fifth century ; and 'neath the wing
Of great St. Germain, Bishop of Auxerre,
    Her holy growth progress'd with rapid spring ;
      The angels of the skies,
        Rejoicing in her birth,
      Therein did recognise
        A sister come on earth ;

And so they made a rare
  " Fête extraordinaire,"
They set the planets whirling
  In mazy dance,
  All over France,
Like girls that follow Girling ;
  Angelic lights
  (So Giry writes)
Jump'd thro' the clouds quite frisky,
  As if the Deuce
  Had broken loose,
And taken—too much whisky !

II.

To such a grand *début*,
Her after life was true ;
  And meek, devout, and grave,
And full of holy fire
And spiritual desire
  Was sweet young Geneviève.
At fifteen years of age
The Maid began to wage
  Her war with sin ;
And training hard and *fast*
(Especially the last),
  She grew quite thin ;
And this is how she train'd,
And stamina obtain'd
  Her cause to win :

On Monday, Tuesday, Wednesday her fare
  Its narrow range
  Would never change,
Consisting totally of praise and prayer ;
  On Thursday night
  A banquet slight
Of stalest bread and beans the Saint partook of ;
  To quench her thirst,
  The very worst
Of water—stuff none else could bear the look of.
  When Sunday came
  'Twas just the same ;
She took one meal so spare and thrifty,
  Tho' since the last
  Three days had pass'd.
Thus lived the maid from fifteen up to fifty.

III.

No wonder by such deeds our Saint's renown
Soon burst the limits of her native town.
At home she was beset with sordid cares,
Her mundane mother saw that her affairs
Domestic suffer'd from the girl's neglect,
To this Gerontia strongly did object,
Forbade her going to church six times a week,
And, on remonstrance, slapp'd her on the cheek :
Such sacrilege unpunish'd could not go,
That slap was answer'd by a harder blow ;
For Dame Gerontia soon was stricken blind,
And for two years in total darkness pined ;

Till, Geneviève, by prayer her sight restored.
Her parents saw they could no more afford
To thwart a child so back'd by heaven's grace :
They let her a monastic life embrace.

IV.

A beldame " came down like a wolf on the fold,"
Stole Geneviève's sandals, so holey and old,
And " toted them home," where this naughty old soul
Became on a sudden as blind as a mole ;
'Twas fearful to witness her horror and fright,
For *blindness* at best is a terrible *sight;*
She took up the shoes, not to sell or to " swop "
With travelling Jew or at pawnbroker's shop,
But back to the owner, and own'd to the theft,
And begg'd for the sense which her vengeance had reft.
Kind Geneviève never such plea could refuse—
" I'll give you your sight if you'll give me my shoes,"
And added, while pulling one on with a strain,
" Mind, don't *put your foot in it* this way again ! "

V.

So fared many more 'gainst the Saint who transgress'd :
One woman—no doubt by the demon possess'd—
With deep curiosity ventured to pry
Where closely concealed from humanity's eye,
The maid had withdrawn to her *sanctum sanctorum.*
The eyes of the spy felt a darkness come o'er 'em,
And not till her saintship came out of her cell
The sinner was freed from the terrible spell ;

That sanctified hand scarce her forehead had cross'd
Ere came in perfection the sight she had lost.
On other occasions did blindness descend
On those who St. Geneviève chanced to offend,
Whilst those, we suppose, who most pleased her, she blest
With sharpness of vision beyond all the rest.

VI.

Success on earth, too well we know,
   Arouseth green-eyed jealousie ;
" Tho' chaste as ice and pure as snow,"
   From slander none are wholly free.
Evil with good its war will wage,
   And till the Right its foe shall quell,
Make earth the Devil's acting-stage,
   The battlefield of heaven and hell :
So Geneviève, so good and pure,
   Was even branded as imposter,
And ere she made her footing sure
   What pain and anguish did it cost her !
But virtue in the end must win,
   However sinners may resist,
Anon the maid rejoicèd in
   The love of every pietist ;
Pupils were placed beneath her care,
   And nuns she train'd in holy ways,
While godly people everywhere
   Pronounced her name with reverent praise :
Far nations saw with great content
   The heavenly radiance that did fill her,

And our old friend Stÿlites sent
   His blessing—*posted* at his *pillar*.

VII.

The virtues of St. Geneviève,
   Her power and fame among the French,
So made the devil fume and rave,
   He long'd her holy star to quench ;
He *did* put out her candle's light,
   And when she came, the church was dark ;
She touch'd the wick, which soon was bright
   Relumed as by some heavenly spark,
For Geneviève possess'd the gift
   Of making fire by touch alone :
Such privilege conduced to thrift,
   For May and Bryant were unknown,
Tho' *Lucifer*, call'd otherwise "Old Scratch,"
   Burnt freely, yet he seldom found his *match*.

VIII.

The devil he sat on a flask of oil,
   A practical joke loved he,
And deem'd all mortals his lawful spoil ;
   So laugh'd to himself in glee,
To think of the girl who carried the cruet ;
   "O wouldn't she drop me and run if she knew it !"
For he wore his best invisible coat ;
   But soon he alter'd his joysome note—

A little way off from his moving perch
   St. Geneviève stood at the door of her church,
And Satan trembled in every limb,
   For Geneviève's eyes were *fix'd on him.*
"What hast thou?" she of the child did ask,
   "Most holy abbess, some oil in a flask."
Then Geneviève raised her saintly hand,
   The bottle in pieces smash'd,
The fluid spilt on the thirsty sand,
   And the fiend flew off abash'd ;
Then merely by words the potent Saint
   Restored the vessel whole.
Refill'd and blest, lest the evil taint
   Might peril the bearer's soul ;
(How many of us unknowing carry,
How few can behold, and resist, Old Harry !)
And thus, the Evil One's game to spoil,
St. G., with opportune blow, *struck oil.*

IX.

When in her honour they erected
   The church that still upholds the name
Of Geneviève, an unexpected
   Misfortune on the builders came,
Their liquor fail'd.   What could they do?
   For labour ever is athirst,
And in such daily workers' view
   Drought is of evils far the worst.

ST. GENEVIEVE AND THE DEMON.　A FRENCH *EXORCISE*.

They came to HER ; she pray'd and *tapp'd*
  A huge jar with her fingers fine,
And lo !" ane merveillous thynge there happ'd
  The vase at once was fill'd with wine !
And till the fane was rear'd aloft
  That blessed "tap" was never out ;
The workmen drank "as much and oft
  As they inclined." I greatly doubt
If such a plan would prosper *here*
  With British workmen and their beer.

X.

But 'midst her many miracles of mercy and of might,
The saving of her chosen town shines out with brightest
  light.
When dreadful Attila the Hun, with all his savage clan,
Who call'd himself the "Scourge of God," and *was* the
  scourge of man,
Swoop'd like a vulture down on Gaul, and murder'd, robb'd,
  and sack'd.
Poor Paris very naturally feared to be attack'd.
A panic seized the city, and its burgesses resolved
By timely fleeing to avoid the ruin thus involved.
But earnestly their patroness restrain'd and calmed their
  fears,
And bade them soften Heaven's wrath with penitential tears ;
And tho' the Devil stirr'd them up to murmur and oppose,
And even threaten her with death, she triumph'd o'er all
  foes ;

Her prayers prevail'd, the city 'scaped a climax so distressful,
Whilst in the other parts of Gaul the Huns were *Huns*-suc-
    cessful,
Altho' their numbers seem'd to give their opponents no
    chance,
The Romans, Franks, and Visigoths expell'd them all from
    France ; .
To Geneviève 'twas very plain this miracle was owing,
It set the flower of her fame " a-blowing and a-growing."

XI.

Five years of safety passed, and then
King Merovèe, with all his men,
Long down before Lutetia sate,
And nought could now avert her fate,
For she was doom'd, by Heaven's decree,
The world's " gay capital " to be,
So Paris fell, but Geneviève
Still like an angel did behave ;
She could not save it from the Franks,
But she could earn a nation's thanks,
And blessings by her pious deeds
Of ministration to their needs.
Fell Famine, with its grisly touch,
Soon *thinn'd* the population much,
So off she started up the Seine,
In neighbouring parts to gather grain,
And here a miracle befell
Which briefly I proceed to tell.

XII.

Beneath the stream there grew a tree,
(*How* it came there perplexeth me),
And on its branches gnarl'd and jagg'd
Unlucky boats were often " snagg'd,"
And all their passengers and freight
Involved in one destructive fate.
The Saint, whose vessel near'd the spot,
Was threaten'd with the common lot ;
Two hideous heads of giant size
Sudden from out the waves did rise.
Such *Spirits* then were *strong* in *water.*
These in their clutches nearly caught her,
But she, defying their attacks,
Pray'd and commanded that the axe
Should to the tree's foul roots be laid.
'Twas done ; the monsters fled dismay'd,
And from that day the stream was clear ;
Nor did the spirit's re-appear.
(P.S. This miracle, as *some* maintain,
Occurred upon the coast of Spain.)

XIII.

Soon back in triumph Geneviève was borne,
Bringing eleven boats well cramm'd with corn ;
To her it was enjoyment most intense
This food to starving sufferers to dispense ;
She even baked the bread herself, and drew
Some out half-baked to feed the weaker few

(Under the rose) ; yet when the batch was finish'd
'Twas found the tale of loaves was undiminish'd.
One other wondrous deed will I detail,
Then haste to close, for space begins to fail.

XIV.

King Chilpèric 'twas vain to seek,
   For none knew where to find him,
From Paris gay he had sneak'd away,
   And shut the gates behind him.
That king had doom'd twelve men to die—
We do not know exactly why—
But France had then a full supply
   Of crime and immorality ;
The monarch had preferr'd to leave,
Lest Geneviève (or " Jenny Veeve ")
Should come and beg for a reprieve,
   Averting the fatality.
She learnt the fact, and quickly went,
The king's design to circumvent,
And triumph in the good intent
   She carried out so trustily.
She reach'd the gate, St. Martin hight,
But there the warder impolite
Her plea refused, still kept it tight,
   And growl'd at her most crustily ;
But soon that warder changed his tone,
When wide the gate was open thrown,
And unseen angels laid him prone,
   And made him bellow lustily.

With mighty helpers such as these,
What needed she the aid of keys?
St. Geneviève released with ease
　The culprits from their durance,
And then she sought and found the king,
And managed him to terms to bring,
And give consent to everything
　That wrought their lives' insurance.

XV.

No saint in all the calendar
Carried her healing powers so far
As Geneviève, tho' no degree
She held of surgeon or M.D.
She cured the blind, as we have told,
And ailments half a lifetime old,
And madness nothing could withstand,
All melted 'neath her gentle hand,
Those " shocks to which the flesh is heir "
She never look'd on with despair,
A child, who once to see her came,
Was deaf, and dumb, and blind, and lame,
And " past all surgery " one would think,
Yet did the patroness not shrink
From such a case ; her prayers were heard,
Her sacred oil administer'd,
And soon the child began to talk,
To hear, and see, and jump, and walk ;
Nay, Geneviève, 'tis even said,
Could raise up those already dead ;

D

As instanced by a child who fell
With fatal force into a well,
But whom the Saint's all-healing power
Restored to life in half-an-hour.

XVI.

The virgin Saint was now grown rather *passée*
　(Most ladies are at eighty-three or so),
And had she deign'd to stand before a *glass*, a
　Reflection sad that glass had had to show ;
For beans and bread, and vigils, tears and fasting,
　Are apt to fail—if beauty be their goal,
But they develop what is far more lasting,
　A starving body makes a fatted soul,
No wonder she was very often ailing ;
　When we observe how all her life she cried,
Her own and other people's sins bewailing,
　It seems no wonder that at last she died.
　　　For she was ever prone to weep
　　　　And weep with right good-will
　　　Awake she cried with sadness deep
　　　　Asleep she sorrow'd still ;
　　　Her chamber-floor was like a sea,
　　　　Its boards her tears did drench,
　　　She was a second Niobe
　　　　Translated into French ;
　　　It could not, could not last
　　　　Such anguish unremitting,
　　　Her sainted spirit pass'd
　　　　To regions more befitting.

She died, and then—O dear !
What sorrow was created,
The town went mad with sheer
Grief unadulterated.

XVII.

It was about the year of grace 500
Her soul from clayey tenement was sunder'd,
Her heavenly passport was made out and sign'd
Ere in the tomb her body was enshrined,
But miracles began almost before
Her soul had time to knock at Peter's door ;
Cured were the mad and sick and blind and lame,
All other physic quite a " drug " became,
And those who tried the panacea were fain
To own that *now* " physicians were in vain."
The wealth upon her shrine exceeds belief,
Until it was " annex'd " by midnight thief :
Upon the tomb where lies this best of women,
'Tis said there shines a lamp which needs no trimming,
And fills itself—precluding care and cost—
With sacred oil which nothing can exhaust,
The oil's, too, ta'en for healing, yet the flame,
Like Parsee fires, keeps burning on the same ;
Well o'er the dust may miracles be rife
Of one who did such wonders all her life,
That Giry makes subtraction from their sum—
" A cause de *l'incrédulité* des hommes ;"
Which candid statement proves such wonders owe
Much to the kind of soil on which they grow.

'Tis certain, tho' Munchausen's self should weave them
All tales are true—*to those who can believe them.*

So now you've learnt the life and deeds
   Of Geneviève the good,
Own that her merit far exceeds
   Most saints' in magnitude ;
Her blessed memory all should hail
   With metaphoric laurel,
Thus, reader, I've " adorn'd the tale,"
   I pr'y thee " point the moral."

No. 6—ST. DENYS OF FRANCE (A.D. 272).

N.B.—The four following lays are composed in humble imitation of the popular bards of Transatlantica.

WHICH I mean to observe—
 And my statement is true—
  That for ways that unnerve,
And for deeds that out-do,
St. Denys of France was peculiar,
 And the same I'll explain unto you.

Dionysius his name,
 And none will deny
That Denys the same
 Does mean and imply ;
And he fell in the hands of the pagans,
 Who doom'd him a martyr to die.

'Twas century third,
 As the history states,
'That Denys incurr'd
 This saddest of fates ;
With one Eleutherius, deacon,
 And Rusticus, priest, for his mates.

Yet the woes that were laid
  On those Christians three,
And the pluck they display'd
  Were quite frightful to see,
And at first you would scarcely believe it,
  But the same is asserted by ME.

'Twas one of their foes'
  Diabolical whims,
To the flames to expose
  The martyr's bare limbs.
But Denys, for one, didn't mind it,
  He lay and sang psalms—likewise hymns.

And then he was placed
  In a den of wild beasts
With a preference of taste
  For martyrs and priests ;
But Denys, by *crossing*, so tamed them.
  They turned from such cannibal feasts.

Next Denys was cast
  In a furnace of fire ;
All thinking at last
  He'd have to expire ;
But the flame sank so low in a minute,
  No bellows could make it rise higher.

And when he'd been hung
  On the cross for a spell,
St. Denys was flung
  With his friends in a cell,
As narrow and close as a coffin,
  And dark as H E double L.

Said the judge, stern and curt,
  " Bring the captives to me."
When he found them unhurt
  He cried, " Can this be ?
We are ruin'd by Christian endeavour ; "
  And he meant to destroy the whole three.

On the Saints, who had long
  Withstood such attacks,
The foe came out strong
  With their tortures and racks.
At last, by the Governor's order,
  Their heads were cut off with an axe.

" Do we sleep ? do we dream ? "
  All the witnesses shout ;
" Are men what they seem ?
  Or is witchcraft about ?"
For quickly the corpse of St. Denys
  Rose up, and began to walk out !

He took up his head,
    Tuck'd it under his arm,
And the same, it is said,
    Caused surprise and alarm ;
Each eye on the marvel was fasten'd
    As if by some magical charm.

Cut down to his neck,
    Like a flower to its stalk,
The Saint met a check
    When he first tried to walk :
But soon he felt stronger than Weston
    Or Webb—by a very long chalk.

And angels, we're told,
    Led his footsteps along ;
While heavenwards rolled
    Their chorus of song ;
They led him two leagues from the city,
    To see that he didn't go wrong.

I hope you'll believe
    That this story is fact,
For I scorn to deceive,
    And refuse to retract ;
For truth I've a great reputation,
    And wish to preserve it intact.

ST. DENYS'S "PREMIER PAS."

Which is why I observe—
    Aod my statement is true—
That for ways that unnerve,
    And for deeds that out-do,
St. Denys of France was peculiar,
    And the same I have proved unto you.

No. 7—SISTER BEATRICE (A.D. uncertain).

THIS is the metre Columbian. The soft-flowing
   trochees and dactyls,
   Blended with fragments spondaic, and here and
   there an iambus,
Syllables often sixteen, or more or less, as it happens,
Difficult always to scan, and depending greatly on accent,
Being a close imitation, in English, of Latin hexameters—
Fluent in sound, and avoiding the stiffness of commoner
   blank verse,
Having the grandeur and flow of America's mountains and
   rivers,
Such as no bard could achieve in a mean little island like
   England ;
Oft, at the end of a line, the sentence dividing abruptly
Breaks, and in accents mellifluous follows the thoughts of the
   author.

I.

In the old miracle days, in Rome the abode of the saintly,
To and fro in a room of her sacred conventual dwelling,
Clad in garments of serge, with a veil in the style of her
   Order,
Mass-book and rosary too, with a bunch of keys at her
   girdle,
Walk'd, with a pensive air, Beatrice the Carmelite sister.

Fair of aspect was she, but a trifle vivacious and worldly,
And not altogether cut out for a life of devout contempla-
tion.
More of freedom already had she than the rest of the
sisters,
For her s was the duty to ope the gates of the convent, and
take in
Messages, parcels, *et cetera*, from those who came to the
wicket.
Ever and often she paused to gaze on the face of Our Lady,
Limn'd in a picture above by some old pre-Raphaelite
Master ;
Then would she say to herself (because there was none else
to talk to),
" Why should I thus be immured, when people outside are
enjoying
Thousands of sights and scenes, while I'm not allowed to
behold them,
Thousands of joys and of changes, while I am joyless and
changeless ?
No, 1 can stand it no longer. I'll hasten away from the
Convent :
Now is the time, for all's quiet ; there's no one to see or to
catch me."
So resolving at length, she took off her habit monastic,
And promptly array'd herself in smuggled secular garments ;
Then on the kneeling-desk she laid down the keys, in a safe
place,
Where some one or other, or somebody else, would certainly
find them.

"Take thou charge of these keys, blest Mother," then mur-
    mured Beatrice,
"And guard all the nuns in this holy but insupportable
    building."
And as she spoke these words, the eyes of the picture were
    fasten'd
With mournful expression upon her, and tears could be seen
    on the canvas ;
Little she heeded, however, her thoughts had played truant
    before her,
Then stole she out of the portal, and never once looking
    behind her,
Wrapp'd in an ample cloak, and further concealed by the
    darkness,
Out through the streets of the city Beatrice quickly
    skedaddled.

II.

Out in the world went Beatrice, her cell was left dark and
    deserted ;
Scarce had she gone when lo ! with wonderment best re-
    lated—
Down from her canvas and frame, there stepp'd the blessed
    Madonna,
Took up the keys and the raiment Beatrice had quitted and
    wore them,
Also assuming the face and figure of her who was absent ;
Became in appearance a nun, so that none could know the
    difference,

Save that the sisters agreed that Beatrice the portress was
　　growing
Better and better, as one who aspired to canonization ;
Daily abounding in grace, a pattern to all in the convent ;
Till it would not have surprised them to see a celestial halo
Gather around her head, and pinions sprout from her
　　shoulders,
That, when too good for this world, she might fly away to a
　　better.
Her post was below her deserts, and so by promotion they
　　made her
Mistress of all the novices seeking religious instruction.
Such was her great success in that tender and beautiful
　　office,
Her pupils all bloomed into saints, and some of the very first
　　water.

III.

Many a day had pass'd since Beatrice escaped from the
　　convent,
Much had she seen of the world, and it's wickedness greatly
　　distress'd her ;
Oft she repented her act, and long'd to return, yet she dared
　　not ;
Oft was determined to go, still she "stood on the order of
　　going."
Thus it at last occurr'd that her convent's secular agent
Entered one day, in the house where the truant sister was
　　staying,

But changed as she was in appearance, he did not know her
    from Adam ;
Whilst he in his clerical garb was to her a familiar figure.
" Now I shall learn," thought she, " what they say of my
    flight and my absence."
And so she eagerly asked of the nuns and of sister Beatrice,
As of a friend she had known when living near to the
    convent.
" Truly," the factor replied, " She is still the pride of our
    sisters,
Favourite too of the abbess, and worthy of all our affection.
Would there were more of her kind in *some* houses monastic
    I know of,"
Puzzled, and rather distress'd, then answered the truant
    relegieuse,
" She whom I speak of, alas ! was less of a saint than a
    sinner,
She fled from the veil and the cell, so surely you speak of
    another ? "
" Not in the least, my child," the secular agent responded ;
" Sister Beatrice, the saint-like, did *not* run away from the
    cloister,
Mistress is she of the novices.   Why should she go ?   Stuff
    and nonsense ! "
" What can it mean ? " thought Beatrice, " and who is my
    double and namesake ? "
So when the agent was gone, resolved she would settle the
    question,
Off to the convent she went, and knocked at the portal
    familiar,

Ask'd for the sister Beatrice, was shown to the parlour and
  found a
Counterpart of herself, as she was in her days of seclusion.
Down on her knees went Beatrice—the why and the where-
  fore she knew not.
" Welcome, my daughter, again," said her double, the blessed
  Madonna ;
" Now I restore you your keys, your robe, and your other
  belongings,
Adding the excellent name and promotion I've won in your
  likeness ;
Be you a nun as before, but more pious ; farewell, take my
  blessing."
Speaking, she melted away in the holy pre-Raphaelite
  picture.
Again was Beatrice " herself," like Richard the third, à la
  Shakespeare,
Growing in grace from that day, and winning the glory of
  Saintship ;
While each of the pupils she taught, went to heaven as surely
  as *she* did.

Such is the metre Columbian, but where is the bard who de-
  vised it ?
Tenderest he of the poets who wrote in the tongue of (New)
  England,
Where the minstrel who sang of " Evangeline," also " Miles
  Standish ?"

Alas ! he will never again pour forth his effusions pathetic,
But his name and his fame endure, and this characteristic
    measure
In honour of him I adopt, without any thought of bur-
    lesquing.
Thus on the ear its cadence, like sounds from the labouring
    ocean,
Breaks, and in accents mellifluous follows the thoughts of
    the author.

IT was many and many a year ago,
   In a World they call the New,
   That a maiden there lived whom you may
      know
As the blessed St. Rose of Peru ;
And this maiden she lived with no other thought
   Than the penances she could do.

She was a child, yet never a child
   Did holiness so pursue,
By morning and night, and by candle-light
   In wisdom and grace she grew,
And ever would strive to all earthly faults
   And pleasures to say adieu.

An angel in beauty, she thought it was right
   To spoil it to mortals' view,
She scratch'd it with briars, and burnt it in fires,
   Until she was known by few ;
(O maidens whose charms you but live to adorn
   This never would do for *you !*)

But her fear of the world was more than her fear
   Of loveliness losing its due—
Of tortures that thrill'd her through ;
       E

And neither the sackcloth she wore to her skin,
Nor her spiky belt thereto,
Could ever elicit the faintest complaint
From the blessed St. Rose of Peru.

When Love drew near with its honey'd words,
And tenderly tried to woo,
The name of wife and the joys of life
She rigidly would eschew.
She prick'd, for her sins, her head with pins,
And the blood in streamlets drew,
And tears they were spilt for her fancied guilt,
By the blessed St. Rose of Peru.

And oft she would fast, but to eat at last
The bitterest herbs she knew,
And all that was pleasant and good to the taste
In horror away she threw ;
She stripp'd her garden of all sweet flowers,
And sow'd it with thorns and rue.

And angels would come and make her one
(In dreams) of their seraph crew,
And often the Fiend, in his beauty screen'd,
Her spirit would fain subdue,
But evil could only fail to prevail
With the blessed St. Rose of Peru

And these are the reasons her fame would grow
   In the World they call the New,
But youth wasn't past ere the wintry blast
   The flame of her life out-blew ;
There issued a breath from the mouth of Death
   Chilling and killing the Rose of Peru.

And many and many a year flew by
   In that World they call the New,
While marvels divine were wrought at the shrine
   Of the blessed St. Rose of Peru.
(I should beat my breast and be much distress'd
   If you call'd this part untrue.)

But my teeth never ache but I think, as I wake,
   Of the blessed St. Rose of Peru ;
And my corns never shoot, but the woes I compute
   Of the blessed St. Rose of Peru ;
And so I decide my pangs to abide
   Like her who suffer'd—and braved—and died
      In the capital of Peru,
      The region they call Peru.

No 9.—ST. SMITH OF UTAH (A.D. 1844.)

I.

SONG of the Far West,
    A song of the Great Salt Lake, of Utah, Nauvoo,
    Jackson County, and the new Jerusalem.
Listen, individuals, communities, sects, nations ;
I am (for this occasion only) a Transatlantic bard,
None of your smooth court-poets of worn-out Eurôpian
    monarchies,
But a bird of the backwoods—a loud-throated warbler of the
    forest ;
My inspiration is the breath of the boundless prairie ; my
    mental food is the *roll* of the raging Atlantic.
Rhyme ?—I scorn it. Metre ?—Snakes and alligators ! what
    is that to ME ?
Libertad for ever ! I intend to sing anyhow—and all-how,
    just as I tarnation please.
Universe, are you listening ? very. well, then ; here goes,
    right away.

II.

SMITH ! ! ! !
Smith the Apostle ! ! !
Smith the Evangelist ! !
Smith the Discoverer of the Book of Mormon !
His name was Joseph, and he was raised at Sharon, Windsor,
    County Vermont, U.S.

His parents were tillers of the soil—poor, but dishonest,
When they wanted money, they took it ; horses, they boned
    them ; sheep, they annexed them ;
But saints may spring from sinners, as a butterfly springs
    from a maggot.

III.

Angels ! heavenly visions ! !
In white robes, with crowns, harps, and everything accord-
    ing,
Bless'd the youthful Smith with their presence beatific.
He went into solitude, loafing in caves, backwoods, and
    lonely canyons.
Those angels meant business; thrice in one night they
    sought him.
They told him all his sins were liquidated,
Told him the history of the World (*not* according to Moses)'
Told him the Red Injuns was one of the lost tribes of Israel ;
Told him where to find the sacred book of the Prophet
    Mormon,
Told him to bring it out, and make a good " spec " of the
    business.

IV.

Leap, O my soul, every 22nd of September,
For on that date Smith found the sacred volume !
Eighteen-twenty-seven—a year to be remembered ! ! !
Sheets of tin, with characters antique engraven—
Such was the wondrous Book of Mormon.

From that prophet Smith profited, and became a prophet
    also.
Mahomet, Brahma, Buddha, Confucius—Smith surpassed
    them all.
Getting behind a screen, he dictated to Oliver Cowdrey
(Smith was not a *literatus*, and couldn't have jerk'd it gram-
    matically).
In eighteen-thirty, hurrah ! the glorious Book was publish'd.
But carping critics of orthodoxy murmured "fraud !" and
    "humbug ! "
" Where's your authority.?   Show us the original ! "
Smith disdained to do so ; he and his friends had seen it,
But nobody else has seen it, nor will they see it forever.
Yet did Smith triumph, and gather'd in converts like hay in
    the sunshine.
Virtue will ever prevail, as long as the world circumvolvulates
    on its axis.

V.

Huzza for the New Jerusalem !
At Kirtland, Ohio, Smith with his Saints located,
Till, in March, '32, there came a band of Nonconformists,
Seized Joseph the Saint, and Rigdon his mate, and gave
    them tar and feathers !
O my soul, boil, boil like a potato with indignation !
From county to county, and state to state, for years the Mor-
    mons were driven,
Sometimes camping out 'neath the snow-cold stars of win-
    ter.
At last they found a resting place—Clay county, in Missouri.

Thither came Brigham Young—at that time Brigham
younger.
Smith sent him out to bring to grace those sceptical down-
easters,
Whilst Orson Pratt and Heber C. Kimball were missionaries
in Europe.

VI.

In this world banks will break and promoters be call'd
swindlers :
This was the luck of Smith and his saintly companions—
Lo ! the bank of Kirtland busted, the Mormons were clapp'd
in prison,
Not long afterwards they received this heavenly revelation—
" Missouri's too hot to hold you "—they " vamosed the
ranche," according.

VII.

O, Nauvoo, city of Beauty !
Land of delight, fertility, promise, and blossoming realiza-
tions !
When I beheld thee my soul was enthrall'd, and danced a
spirited *can-can*.
Thither came 15,000 saints, and squatted in glory,
And the desert blossom'd as the rose, beneath the smile of
Smith.
He preach'd the gospel, and got up a government-house and
militia,
Was mayor of the town, high priest, and commander-in-
chief of the army ;

O, *gloria !* triumph ! bravo ! hosannah ! huzza ! halleluiah !
(These are the words of a soul jumping out of its skin with
felicity.)

VIII.

Once more " revelation " came, and spake unto Smith the
prophet.
" The relation between man and woman is not only social
but spiritual.
The social is bounded by two, the spiritual knows of no
limit ;
Wherefore, O Smith, you may take what number of wives
you think proper,
Sanctifying them by sacred mysterious ' sealings.' "
(Redder, seekest thou further to know, then go and consult
Hepworth Dixon.)
But the cold hard world disapproved of spiritual marriage ;
War rose up against Smith, and again, with his mates, he
was cast into prison,
" Revelation " helped them no more ; no, nor did angels
assist them ;
But a gang of rowdies (A.D. 1844) broke into the prison,
Haul'd out Joseph Smith and his brother Hyram,
And with their too-true revolvers they sent them both to
glory !

IX.

Sinners make martyrs, and martyrs make saints (this is
logic).
Smith was a martyr, and mourned by the Mormons according,

Especially Brigham Young, who came in for his fortune and fixtures.

In 1850 they established the Salt Lake City,

And two years later another great "revelation" set up spiritual wifehood, the glorious cause that Smith died for.

Thus, like a beautiful tree, grew up the doctrine of spiritual marriage,

Monogamy, bigamy, trigamy, quadrigamy, quinquigamy, and lastly polygamy—

Till, if you ask me, "How many wives has Brigham?"

I shall answer, "Go, count the waves of the boundless Atlantic!"

X.

They made Smith a saint—a boss saint—and was he not worthy?

Far more than the worn-out Saints of your rotten Eur*ópi*an kingdoms!

Bully for Joseph! my eyes fill with tears; don't yours?

I admire Joe Smith—I *du*—I'll wrap up his memory in lavender,

And if you love me, reader (as I'm sure you cannot help it),

Go thou and do likewise.

XI.

Mourn for Smith; mourn, mourn, ye peoples!

O songsters, bards of all times, climes, regions, and generations,

O warblers, tenori, bassi, contralti, and mezzi-soprani,

O Christian men of every land and language,
O kings, priests, presidents, khans, kaisers, and subjects,
O infinitively diversified inhabitants of this revolving kosmos,
Sing, and sing, and sing, and keep on singing his honour
    and glory,
Echo and re-echo forever the name of Joe Smith, boss Saint
    of the Mormons !

No. 10.—ST. FILLAN'S ARM.

(A LAY OF SCOTT-LAND.)

HARP of the North, that hangs, or used to hang,
　　" On the witch-elm that shades St. Fillan's
　　　spring "
(*Which* elm I know not), wake thy tuneful twang,
　And keep thy wires in order while I sing
In verse of true Sir Walter Scottish ring ;
　And lest your Minstrel's strength should haply faint
Glenlivat shall its inspiration bring ;
　Thus will we make the Sassenach acquaint
With blessed Fillan's life, thy friend and patron Saint.

I.

If thou would'st view old Pittenweem aright,
Go visit it by the broad daylight,
For if the night were murky, pray
How couldst thou ken that fair Abbaye !
And should it eke come on to rain,
Thy pleasure would be turn'd to pain ;
But when the golden sunbeams smile
On ruin'd nave and barren aisle,
When noontide rays enlivening fall
On thistly floor and weedy wall,
So that thou need'st not break thy bones
Or shins against the rugged stones,
Then go ; but take a trusty guide
Who knows the country far and wide,

And give him half-a-crown or so,
To tell thee all that he may know ;
But should he show thee Fillan's tomb
Within some cloister's ivied gloom,
Believe him not, although he swear,
Because the Saint's not buried there.

II.

Breathes there the man who having read
All that the Northern Bard has said,
All the particulars supplied
By travellers' tomes and Murray's Guide,
Of Scotia's landscapes fair and grand,
Longs not to see that favour'd land ?
Oh, would that *I* could get the chance
To view those regions of romance,
What pleasure to be climbing now
Ben Dizzy's stern and lofty brow !
How sweet to stand beside the Frith
That owes its waters to Loch Smith,
To mark Bel-hangar's ruin'd pile,
And Ion-munga's charmed isle,
Whilst in the distance can be seen
The giant peaks of Ben Zoleen,*
And, if the weather be not dull,
The fragrant isle of Sneeshin-Mull ;
And, floating like a mirage there,
That phantom ship, the " *Brig* of *Ayr* "

The writer will not guarantee the absolute correctness of all these names of
localities, but he has carefully consulted the best authorities on the subject.

Sails where Loch Toddy's smile creates
A beauty that intoxicates.
Then view, my fancy, if thou wilt,
Knights tourneying within Glen-*Tilt*,
Hear Roderick Dhu and brave Fitz-James
Calling each other dreadful names,
And see them chase, through bosky dells,
The *hart* that "in the Highlands" dwells.
Oh, if some friend would pay my fare,
How "like a bird" I'd wander there !

III.

The meal was over at Pittenweem ;
The monks had gone to their cells to dream,
Or heavily sleep, as the case might be,
Till waked by the bell at half-past three ;
The Abbot had gone to his private tower,
For *he* sat up till a later hour,
And oft he would have his under-prior
To sit and talk by the cosy fire ;
For Abbots of old, you may suppose,
Could do in such matters as they chose,
And here, from the mill-stream's outer loch
To the tippest top of the weather-cock,
Good Fillan the Abbot ruled supreme—
Such was the custom of Pittenweem.

IV.

The night was long, the weather cold ;
A Minstrel, neither young nor old,
Whose ragged coat and shoes in holes

Wrung pity from those monkish souls,
Entered the Abbey's lower hall,
Whence, duteous to the Abbot's call,
He brought himself and harp upstairs
And 'gan show off his Scottish airs.
It was a charity to bring
Such warbler in the place to sing.
St. Fillan gave him ample cheer
And copious draughts of home-made beer,
Till, while that inspiration work'd,
This music from the wires he jerk'd :—

V.

BALLAD.

THE BLUE BROTHER.

'Twas on Maxwelton's bonny braes
    (" Where early fa's the dew ").
That at the set of sun I met
    A Friar of Orders blue.

With sigh, and frown, and eyes cast down,
    His face was sad to see ;
Some heavy care was settled there—
    Whatever could it be?

" Come hither, come hither, thou Holy Friar,
    Why dost thou look so blue ? "
He answer'd stern— " I've yet to learn
    What that's to do with *you*."

" Wert thou," I asked, "a baron bold,
    Who sought a hermit's lot,
Because thy love so false did prove ?"
    He answer'd, " I was *not*."

" And hast thou fought in distant climes,
   Seen mighty cities fall,
And wounded been a score of times? "
   He answered, " Not at all."

" And did thy true love follow thee,
   In page's garb disguised?
And when thou foundest it was she,
   Say, wert thou not surprised? "

" No true love ever follow'd me
   Thus garb'd ; or if she had,
At once, I ween, I must have seen
   Twas she, and not a lad."

" And did she, stricken by thy side,
    In thy embrace expire? "
" Good gracious ! no—who told you so?
   He *must* have been a liar."

" Or hadst thou wooed some ladye fair,
   And wast about to wed,
But saw or heard that she preferr'd
   Another knight instead?

" And didst thou seek their trysting-place,
   And fiercely slay them both,
And there inter both him and her? "
   " I didn't, on my oath !"

" Or didst thou quarrel with a maid,
   Who loved thee all the time,
And seek a hermitage's shade
   Far in a foreign clime?

" And did the maiden seek thee out,
    Dress'd like a pilgrim-boy ?
And, having found thee safe and sound,
    Die, there and then, for joy ? "

Fire flash'd from that Blue Brother's eye ;
    " 'Tis well," he cried, "for you,
That I'm a Friar, else in mine ire
    Some mischief might I do !

" Why should I tell to such as thou
    The story of my youth ?
My patience is exhausted now,
    Denying each untruth.

" You're right, so far, if you suppose
    I've seen some woes and cares,
But, mark you well, I never tell
    To strangers my affairs."

The vesper-bell rang thro' the dell ;
    Abrupt he sped away,
And not another syllable
    Did to this minstrel say.

And tho' upon Maxwelton's braes
    Since then I've often been,
I know not why, but never I
    Have that Blue Brother seen.

VI.

The Abbot praised the Minstrel's skill,
And gave him siller—better still ;
What wonder that such vagrant men,
Encouraged thus, should come agen ?

For Fillan's heart was warm and large,
He never gave these folks in charge,
And tho' the bagpipe made him groan,
He let his torturer alone.
Well used, I wot, were one and all
Within St. Fillan's Abbey-wall ;
   Even the cats were fed on cream—
   Such was the custom of Pittenweem.

VII.

The virtues of a Saint-elect,
'Tis reasonable to expect
   To marvels will give birth ;
And thus, when Fillan did transcribe
The Scriptures—('mid the monkish tribe
   Of books there was a dearth)—
Forth from his hand (the left) there came
The splendour of a mystic flame,
   Too bright to be of earth ;
'Twas Heaven that interposed, 'tis clear,
For candles then were rather dear,
   And at the best burnt dim ;
But by his hand's celestial light,
St. Fillan wrote both day and night—
   'Twas all the same to him.
Oh ! often when the gas is bad,
I wish St. Fillan's Arm I had ;
   At once I'd bid adieu

F

To paraffin and kerosene,
And meters (save of verse, I ween),
  To moulds and " sixes " too !

VIII.

Good Abbot Fillan, it appears,
Ruled o'er the convent many years,
Till, notwithstanding the esteem
He won from all at Pittenweem,
Tho' loved, respected, and admired,
He from his post at length retired,
And lone his hermitage he made
In far Glenurchy's rugged shade—
A desert valley wild and deep,
Now used as pasturage for sheep,
A vale so dark that people say
There's *nightshade* there throughout the day ;
There blooms the heather, green or brown,
There grass springs *up*, and thistle-*down*,
And there the fox by moonlight lies,
And on his paw the *fox-glove* tries,
And there the timid hare will ring
The *hare-bell* whereof poets sing,
And there the Scottish broom, when new,
Sweeps clean, as *brooms* are bound to do.

IX.

'Twas there St. Fillan fix'd his cell,
In saintly solitude to dwell ;

But *why* he from the world withdrew
No living wight precisely knew ;
To man no word would he let fall ;
He *told* his beads, and that was all,
Boon Nature gave him all he ask'd,
Nor was she thus severely task'd.
Simple his fare, he used to dine
Upon the new-laid *eglantine*,
The mountain *ash* was ready-made,
And scarcely needed pepper's aid,
For fruit there grew, profuse and fine,
Pine-apples on each lofty pine ;
His bread was earth's eternal *crust*,
Water he drank, as all men must
Who love St. Wilfrid, son of Law,
And hate wine, beer, and usquebaugh.

X.

By Fillan's cell a fountain sprang,
With whose renown the country rang.
For in its waves the sick were sure
To realise a perfect cure ;
When duck'd within that holy pool,
And then left out all night to cool,
The imbecile in mind and frame
Both hale and sensible became ;
Whatever *ills* they went to quell,
They always left St. Fillan's *well*—
A well which every one must own
Twas better *not* " to leave alone.''

Thus pass'd our Saint through life's decline ;
He died, six-hundred-forty-nine.
His relics, we may well suppose,
Continually in value rose,
But far beyond the rest did stretch
The price his wondrous Arm could fetch,
Till Caledonia's kings felt blest
That such a treasure they possesst.

XI.

Ages had pass'd ; it was the day
Renown'd in *Bannock*-Burn's lay,
When " Scots wha ha'e wi' Wallace bled,"
Knock'd England's projects on the head.
That in his camp King Robert Bruce
Did hold, according to his use,
A public service to invoke
Heaven's aid against the threaten'd yoke ;
But first from out that proud array,
He called the Abbot of Inchaffray.

XII.

" Go, fetch St. Fillan's holy Arm,
   Good priest of Inchaffray,
For it shall be a sacred charm,
   To help our cause this day,
And when the foe perceive its glow
   Perchance they'll run away."

The Abbot went, and quickly brought
  That relic of the Saint,
In silver casket, fairly wrought
  With figures rich and quaint.
The monarch then his pray'r began,
  But when the case was oped,
Behold ! that sacred talisman
  Had, strange to say, eloped.
Stolen ? Such sacrilegious crime
  Our deepest feelings shocks ;
Besides, they'd wasted prayer and time
  Upon an empty box!

XIII.

Dreadful it was to see the Bruce ;
His rage, I wis, had good excuse,
And if he drew his sword to strike,
Why, who would not have done the like ?
" Woe to the wretch's guilty soul
St. Fillan's blessed Arm who stole !
  'Tis vain to intercede
If e'er I find the culprit out,
For such a crime, beyond a doubt,
  Is *Fillanous* indeed ! "
None spoke—such words might well appal,
Tho' purely innocent were all
  His trusty men in mail ;
But certain witnesses did say
That the old priest of Inchaffray
  Look'd very scared and pale.

Yes, he it was whose faith so weak,
Had caused him hide that blest relique,
Lest by its aid the foe should seek
    In battle to prevail.

XIV.

The King, tho' much inclined to swear,
Resumed his interrupted pray'r,
    When lo ! what wonder's here ?
Uprose the casket's silvern lid ;
Then closed—upon my word it did !
    Tho' no one stood a-near.
It was the Saint, who did replace
That severed Arm within its case,
    Unseen to mortal view ;
And when again the lid was raised
That dazzling hand of glory blazed
    Just as it used to do.
The guilty Abbot, tho' amazed,
    No longer look'd so blue.
" Bear witness," cried the grateful King,
" That if this day should victory bring,
    And set us on our legs,
Upon this very spot of ground
A monastery will I found,
    As sure as eggs are eggs."

XV.

And now thy gaze, good reader, turn
    Where tents are fix'd and watches set :

ST. FILLAN'S ARM AND BRUCE'S ARMY.

Upon the banks of Bannockburn
  The deadly foes are met.
A hundred thousand Saxon men,
Fewer the Scots are three to ten—
  Long odds, I ween and bet !
It boots not I should tell thee how
The parties carried on the row ;
How archers arch'd and billmen bill'd ;
What chiels were wounded, ta'en, and kill'd ;
How clouds of cloth-yard arrows sped
As fatally as balls of lead ;
How Southron fell, and Gael was slain ;
How Scottish Lions' might and main
Were well display'd in driving back
The oft-invading Sassenach ;
How gallant Stuart, Moray, Bruce,
And Keith let all their valour loose,
And James, " the good Sir Douglas " hight,
Did more than wonders in the fight.
If these particulars you need,
Go, fetch your " Works of Scott," and read
" Lord of the Isles," thro' Canto VI.
That Scotland's laddies fought like bricks
Is also known to him who learns
The fiery song of Robert Burns ;
And after such as they have sung,
A meaner bard should hold his tongue.

XVI.

O sceptic reader of my song,
To whom should victory's praise belong?

What render'd Scotland's arm so strong ?
It was no earthly might,
It was not luck, it was not pluck,
Nor skill with which the blow was struck;
'Twas Fillan's Arm of light !
And had the Scots the fray began
Unaided by that talisman,
They must have lost the fight.
But there are no such wonders now ;
This is an age of little faith,
When people would as soon avow
Belief in ghost or wraith,
As think a Saint, alive or dead,
'Gainst solid force could so avail,
That relics brought, or prayer said,
Could turn the battle's scale.

XVII.

Be sure the Bruce did not forget
To render to the Saint his debt.
He raised upon that sacred spot
A priory, and well I wot
No finer ruin could be seen
'Twixt John o' Groat's and Aberdeen.
At least, I deem such verdict just,
Tho' purely taken upon trust ;
For long ere this you must have found
I never was on Scottish ground.
More spots than I have time to name
Bear witness to St. Fillan's fame ;

There is "St. Fillan's" near Loch Earn,
In Fife, "St. Phillan's," so I learn ;
There is " Kinfillan " in Renfrew,
" Strathfillan," and within its view,
" Dunfillan," where the orthodox
Show there are hollows in the rocks,
Worn by his knees in constant pray'r.
There also is " St. Fillan's Chair."
And more than one " St. Fillan's Fount "
May enter into this account,
Which further would your time engage,
By *Fillan* up another page.

Harp of the North, farewell ! I'm getting tired
  Of this my theme (and so's the reader too).
Now faints the fervour in my brain, inspired
  By sipping Caledonia's " mountain dew."
Sweet harp ! I'll also give what's *due* to you,
  Assister of my nightin*gaelic* lay ;
Thy wizard wires I tenderly unscrew,
  And hang thee o'er St. Fillan's fountain grey,
Whose story we have told.   So, Minstrel harp, good day

LL know St. George is England's Saint,
    And patron of chivalric fighters,
    And that he slew a dragon grim,
But little more is said of him
    By any ultra-modern writers.

Yet was he of such wide renown,
    That tho' described of Cappadocia,
His fame was early spread of yore
To every part of Levant's shore,
    From Alexandria to Croatia.

To Palestine he came in youth,
    (He owned some land within that region),
And then took up the warrior's trade
With such success, that he was made
    Tribune, and leader of a legion.

He changed his faith—a parlous act
    In his political position—
For 'gainst the Christians then there raged
Fierce war, by Diocletian waged,
    So Georgius threw up his commission,

Gave all his wealth, assumed the Cross,
    And as a missionary started ;
In this he prospered much and long,
Till those in heathendom most strong
    Like vengeful dragons on him darted.

Small mercy had the men who gave
  To idol-worship their adhesion.
By them the saintly George was brought
To Provost Dacyen, one who wrought
  The harsh decrees of Diocletian.

In vain upon the Saint were turn'd
  The terrors of their Inquisition ;
He to his creed adhered as fast
As barnacle to ship—at last
  The Provost called in his Magician,

Who mix'd some wine with poison strong
  To kill, since they could not convert him.
George took the bowl, nor did he shrink
From tossing off the fatal drink ;
  But, strange to say, it didn't hurt him.

They made it stronger, still he drank,
  Nor show'd the slightest signs of dying,
Then, seeing miracles so rife,
The Wizard and the Provost's wife
  Turn'd Christians—which was very trying

To Dacyen, who had torture-wheels,
  With scythes to cut their flesh in pieces,
They plunged him, too, in molten lead,
And yet he was no nearer dead—
  His life seemed held on sev'ral leases.

Till, finding torture would not do,
    The Provost fain must try—persuasion ;
He deemed that method took effect,
So made the populace collect
    Together for this great occasion.

When lo ! recanting not, the Saint
    Pray'd Christian pray'rs—and what was stranger,
Avenging flames from Heaven did fall
On temple, idols, guests and all—
    The Pagans fled in dread and danger.

Now Dacyen, fearful of such might,
    Conceived a final fell intention :—
" I see we must decapitate
This man "—(*that* seem'd the only fate
    Exempt from heavenly intervention).

'Twas done ; upon the morrow's morn,
    A martyr's fate the Bishop suffer'd ;
His tomb's at Ramis, where, 'tis said,
Each pilgrim who was said was " off his head "
    By touching that his " wyttes " recover'd.

St. George was held in great esteem,
    Made patron of Genoa and Britain ;
He reappeared in spectral form
And helped Jerusalem to storm,
    Insuring victory—so 'tis written.

Of England's Order of St. George
  Chivalrous Edward was the starter,
But thro' that doubtful anecdote
Which 'tis not needful here to quote,
  The Order was renamed the Garter.

Our champion's image decks that coin
  Which values twenty times a shilling,
Fighting in most heroic state ;
And now I must in full relate
  The story of his dragon-killing.

He to Sylene's city came
  When folks were in a dreadful hobble,
A dragon dread, whose very breath
Was rife with pestilence and death,
  Had come the citizens to góbble.

They gave, to " soothe its savage breast,"
  Two sheep a-day, till, none remaining,
A sheep and man, then men alone,
No soul could call his life his own,
  And naught was heard but sad complaining.

To kill a dragon was a feat
  No armies ever could succeed in ;
Champions alone in Heaven-sent strength
And courage, could prevail at length—
  This fact all legends are agreed in.

And tourists even now are shown—
  To prove the dragon was no fable—
The well that served as his retreat,
Whence he emerged those meals to eat
  Which needed neither cloth nor table.

So men and women, girls and boys,
  Were gulp'd within that dragon's swallow,
Until 'twas requisite to bring
The only daughter of the king,
  The common fate in turn to follow.

The king wept sore—(he would, you know),
  And pray'd them spare his child for pity ;
" No, sire, the law for all's the same,
And why should'st thou exemption claim ?
  The maid must die to save the city."

Eight days' reprieve—no champion came,
  Till further hope 'twas vain to cherish ;
" Yes, she must die ! "—Oh, sentence sad !
Of course, for lowlier girls 'twas bad,
  But worse for a princess to perish.

They took the royal maid and bound
  Her to a stake to be devour'd ;
And tho' so sore her friends bewail'd,
The girl's own courage never fail'd—
  She was not what you call a coward.

The king gave up his child for lost,
   And all condoled in his bereavement.
'Twas now St. George arrived by chance.
O muse of SPENSER'S sweet romance,
   Aid me to sing this great achievement !

Ye Legende of St. George and ye Dragone.

> " Ye Champioun meeteth ye Princesse
> All readie dight for deth,
> Her doth he reskew, and ye dred-
> Full Dragon vanquisheth.

     *   *   *   *   *

DEEM not, faire dame, quoth then ye gentle knighte,
   Whose hart was piersèd with her piteous case,
That I wolde leeve thee in soe great despight,
   Like recreant knave, or caitive lowe and bace ;
   Certes, I'le meet this dragonne face to face,
And whan he commeth forthe on thee to lunch,
   No haire uppon thine hed shal he displace,
Or chawe thy beateous bones with greedie scrunche,
Ere that, ye monstre's grizly head I'll featlie punche !

Scarce had he said, whan, lo ! with dredfull rore
   As Aetna gives, when bad in its insyde,
Which shooke the erthe for thirty leagues or more,
   Ye hell-born beest approaching they espyde,
   Its winges as windmill's sayles all wagging wyde,
And curling folde on folde its scaylie tayle,
   When as, uprearing high, askaunce it eyed
Ye roiall female and ye knightly male,
In size and bulke it eke was veray lyke a whayle.

His horrid hed, and sparckling armured cote,
  As some infernall crocodyle's did shyne,
His voyce like musicke playing out of note,
    When instruments discordious doe combine ;
    His teeth glemed out in grinning loathlie line,
His eyne like brenning lomps of Walsende cole,
    His mugge so vast and wide, I wel opine,
An oliphaunt he might have swallow'd whole,
He was, in soothe, ynough to fryghten anie lyving sole.

Soon as his blazing orbes on that Princesse
  Ye monstre fixt, than 'gan he to attacke,
Entent to chaw her into nothingnesse
    Within his cavern mowthe so foule and blacke ,
    But when, for better spryng, ye feende drew backe,
Her doughtie Champion, urged by corage stoute,
    His swerde uprist, and delt so shrewde a cracke
Uppon ye tender portion of his snowte,
That from ye wounde a gorie streme rusht redlie out.

Thereat ye dragonne rais'd a gruesome yelle,
  More lowd than twentie gunnes of Armstrong's make,
And on St. George in raging furie felle,
    Forgatt ye hongre hee had com to slake
    On that Princesse, now loost from perlous stake
Wel that ye warriour was so stout of limb,
    Mounted on barb so brave it ne'er could quake,
Enmayled, and ful of corage to ye brimme,
Else had that scaylie brute soone spyfflicated him !

They closed again, for eche was loth to yield,
  Ye feendish beest thrust forth his spightfull clawe,
And fix'd his talaunts in ye Champion's shielde,
    Which rent in twain, that knighte had been yslawe,

ST GEORGE AND THE IM-"MEMORIAL" DRAGON.

But eftly skypping back, he did withdrawe;
Next, on its tonge, he strook a sturdie buffe,
  Making ye dragonne holde his bleedynge iaw,
And as ye Scottische Tyraunt to Macduffe,
He might have cryde for mercie, "holde! ynoughe!"

Eftsoones ye speare empiersed ye dragonne's eie,
  Ye which so moche did raize his yrefull gorge,
He shooke the ayre with manie a salvage crie,
  And with sharpe clutche essay'd to grabbe St. George;
  Now gleem'd his eie like fyre from Volcan's forge,
His verie breth bothe knyghte aud hors knockt downe,
  But uppe they rist, retourning to ye charge;
Our Paladin then crackt ye monstre's croune,
As fiers as Christen trewe attacking fals Mahoune.

Five hours by village clocke had George yfoughte,
  Withouten bytte or suppe his forse to feed,
Yet in those tymes of eld such feats were noughe,
  Ye knightes of yore no provender did need,
  When harte and sowle ingaged in dowtie deede;
Thinke on ye Red Crosse Knighte, in Spenser's lay,
  Three daies unfed, with woundes to smarte and bleed,
He smott a dragonne he had vow'd to slay,
Whereas St. George had onlie foughte ye beest a single day.

Til, whilst eche byrde its dayly song did hushe,
  Ye iolly sunne went publicklie toe bedde,
Whereat ye modest skeys made crimsonne blush,
  While drowsie night her sable curtin spredd;
  And he, our knighte, albe his woundes so bled,
Yet stil his blowes he gave so sharpe and hard,
  Ye dragon, faint with losse, was nearlie ded,
His scayles all chipt, his bodie pierst and scarred,
And so at last he fel ful lengthe uppon ye swarde.

G

Come forthe, bell-dame, quoth then ye gentle knighte,
　And fear no more ye dragonne fiers and cruell,
By Heaven its grace, and my so valiannt myghte,
　Ye monstrous animale hath gotte its gruelle.
　Give me thy girdell wrought with gold and jewell,
Therwith its necke I wil enchaine and clog,
　No mo its eyne doe gleme lyke brenning fuelle,
Ye heest is queld as meeke as anie dogge,
Lead thou it hence, whyle backe we to ye citie jogge.

How merveilled all that wondrous sight to vew !
　Ye seelie folke gan bolt with all their myghte ;
Turn, cried St. George, untoe ye faith that's trewe,
　And then this feende shal doe ye no despight ;
　But if ye treat my words with scornful slight,
Your bones to polpe ye dragon shall devour :
　Attonce upon their sowles came holie light,
And Christen vertues in their hartes did flower,
So thousands were baptysde within that self-same hour.

Now did our knighte cut off ye dragon's hed,
　And had it rais'd aloft that all mought see,
Whereas they knew ther enimie was ded,
　They hugg'd eche other in their hight of glee,
　And unto him who did ye monstre slee,
No mortall threasure semed too great to give ;
　Which then St. George bestow'd in charitee,
On such as in distresse were fain to live,
And showts and blessings did he for that boone receive.

And when ye kynge reclaim'd his doughter dear,
　Whome never he had hoped to see again,
His hart with ioy was fill'd and gladsome cheare.
　He saith to George, " Fair sonne, I pray remaine,

And 'after me ore this wide reaulme rayne,
Taking my child in wedlocke's happie tye."
  " I thancke thee wel," ye champion 'gain explain,
" But, certes, I have other fische to frye,
And at to-morrow's daun 'tis meet I say good-hye."

Ye knighte departed as ye morning came,
  Ye citie mourning much to see him goe,
For by his deed, wel worthe eternall fame,
  Their gratefull love for reskew did they owe,
  And eke that they ye Christen faith did knowe ;
So fared he forthe, to wage more war with ill,
  Alas ! such valoure we behold no mo !
For, tho', perchance, live men of hart and will,
They kill no dragonnes, for ther ben non left to kill.

Some writers steadfastly maintain
  This pretty story's but a fiction,
That dragon's but a type of sin,
And sceptics, when they once begin,
  Play havoc with each old conviction.

Their version makes our doughty Saint
  But one amongst unwarlike sinners,
Whose martial fame did first arise
From his contracting for supplies
  Of meat for Cæsar's soldiers' dinners !

He swindled, too, thro' thick and thin,
  Alike in quality and measure,
And like a wordling base, grew rich
By following but one end, the which
  Was simply his own gain and pleasure.

His peculations roused at last
   The vengeance of the men he cheated,
They would have slain him, but he fled
(Money and all) ere blood was shed ;
 'And none knew where he had retreated.

When lo ! from danger and disgrace,
   On fortune's highest tide he floated ;
As Christian priest was sanctified,
Then took the winning Arian's side,
   Toadied their chiefs, and got promoted.

St. Athanasius—he whose creed
   Some Protestants still disap*prove* of—
Was Egypt's Primate of that hour ;
But soon St. George's growing power
   Caused him to be deposed and *move* off.

So Bishop George in Egypt reign'd,
   With tyrant grasp his sceptre swaying
O'er heathen, heretic, and Jew ;
His wealth by trade and taxes grew,
   Whoever lost, *his* game was paying.

But golden days will never last,
   Constantius died—our " Saint's " upholder,
Apostate Julian ruled the roast,
He turn'd the Primate from his post,
   And gave him a cold cell—and shoulder.

But for the people's just revenge
   The course of law was too protracted ;
And so they stormed the jail forthwith,
And as the Yankees served Joe Smith,
   The Libyans to St. Georgius acted.

In short they lynched the tyrant priest,
   Who caught a well-deserved Tartar ;
But dying in his Church's cause,
She afterwards slipped in her clause,
   To change the sinner to a martyr.

Of course St. George was never here—
   England, perhaps, he scarcely heard of—
But England's knights from Syria brought
Such tales of how he taught and fought
   As no one now believes a word of.

And so they chose him for their Saint,
   Their war-cry and chief benefactor,
Amazed would they have been to know
That the great Saint they honour'd so
   Was but—a rascally contractor !

I hope *this* story is a lie,
   The other version's far more pleasant ;
I hope St. George the dragon slew,
That all his other deeds were true,
Tho' nothing now to me or you,
   And so we'll leave him for the present.

No. 12.—ST. DAVID OF WALES.

 PATRON Saint of Wales,
   Whose month is March, whose emblem is the leek,
   Assist me while I speak—
   Not of those ancient superstitious tales
Our fathers held as truth,
Not legends dear to castle-building youth,
But facts that none can doubt,
Which have in Cambria's history *leek'd* out ;
Great is the Truth, and evermore prevails,
O Patron Saint of Wales !

Sweet land of " Llans," of lakes, and woods, and mountains;
Green vales and fairy fountains,
Rocks, cairns, and Druid-stones,
And towns where everybody's name is Jones.
In other days
I've view'd thy beauties with enraptured gaze,
And even tried in vain
Thy most mellifluous language to attain ;
Yes, Cambria, I love thee, and desire
Awhile to change my lyre
For thy time-honour'd Harp, for now my lay's
In good St. David's praise.

This very holy man
Was son of Xantus, Prince of Cardigan,
And eke (exalted birth could go no farther)
Uncle to great King Arthur.
They prophesied his birth
Some thirty years before he came on earth.
His mother's name was Nun,—
  An appellation
  Which plainly mark'd her for canonization.
She afterwards was sainted like her son.

In miracle, in heavenly miracle,
St. David's life began,
And miracle, continuous miracle,
Throughout the woof of his existence ran,
Continuing when he'd closed his earthly span.
  He early was ordain'd,
And sent to study at the Isle of Wight,
  Thence, when he had remain'd
Long basking in a "dim religious light,"
Came forth from his seclusion,
  And into Wales did carry
  Glad tidings in the guise of missionary,
Putting all heathen notions to confusion.
Few have succeeded
In evangelic work so well as *he* did.

Girald' Cambrensis
Believed in much that contradicts our senses,
Merely remarking, when he has to tell
Something incredible,—

"This fact seems most remarkable to me."
Just read, and you'll agree :
One day St. David's monks together met,
Complain'd they could not get
Sufficient water for each holy rite ;
The Alun's stream was slight
And sluggish, and in thirsty summer weather
It dried up altogether ;
At best its waters were but rank and muddy.
    Our wonder-working Saint,
    On hearing their complaint,   .
Gave to the matter his intensest study ;
Then rose, and to the cemetery went,
And many an hour he spent
In prayer devout.   Of course 'twas heard and granted ;
    Up sprang a crystal fount,
    Unstinted in amount
Of purest lymph—exactly what was wanted.

Once by his power divine
St. David made a brooklet run with wine,
And by his holy spell
The waters of his consecrated well
Were changed—we know not how—
To milk as fresh as any from the cow !
It may be safely stated
Such sacred drinks were unadulterated—
Not as we have them now
" Doctor'd " beyond all cure.
Ah ! to the pure *few* things indeed are pure !

ST. DAVID CHANGES WATER INTO *REAL MILK*.

So holy was St. David,
So little by the Evil One enslavèd,
He always had an angel to attend him,
Befriend him, and defend him,
Inspiring every thought, and word, and act,—
  So runs the story ;
  I know not if 'tis meant for allegory
Or sober fact.
Jackdaws, and crows, and rooks were wont to
    perch
Upon St. David's church,
And, fearing no attack
From grave monastic gentlemen in black,
Lived hapily together
With them, for they were bipeds of one feather ;
And pretty pigeons cooed
Secure in that conventual solitude.
  When strangers would molest
  Those birds, or take a nest,
Some supernatural punishment ensued.

'Twas in the year five hundred and nineteen,
In Brevi's valley green,
That all the holy ones of Wales assembled
(How Satan must have trembled !)
In synod 'neath the Druid oaks umbrageous,
  A fierce crusade to wage
Against the great arch-heretic Pelagius,
  That nightmare of the Faith in that dark age,
Whose wicked power had become outrageous.

Llandevi-brevi was the place's name,
  A sound quite smooth and tame
Compared with syllables like Llanfairfechan,
  Or Ysttradfellte, county Brecon,
Or, still more trying to each vocal organ,
  Llanychaiarn
  Llanllwchalarn
Llanchwg and Castell Llwchwr in Glamorgan.

O'er all the priestly throng
St. David's influence was very strong ;
  His eloquence, his learning,
  His faith so bold and burning,
Won their regard and widen'd his repute ;
  And when he'd spoken
Pelagianism's back was quickly broken.
His miracles assisted to confute :
There was a child lay dead—
What mortal could restore the spirit fled ?
  St. David said, " We'll see,
I will not brag, but bring the child to me."
  They did ; he pray'd,
And on its corse his potent fingers laid.
  The child awoke once more,
Better in health than it had been before.
  Then, while St. David preach'd of faith and
    love,
  There came a snow-white dove,
And perch'd familiarly on his shoulder,
Surprising each beholder.

All saw at once, enlighten'd by religion,
   It was his angel friend,
   Whom Heaven in feather'd form did send,
And not a common pigeon.

These wonders once begun
Were plainly meant for a continuous run.
The child whom he had rescued from the dead
A spotless napkin spread
Upon the ground 'neath David's sacred feet,
   When lo ! that ground rose high,
Up ! up ! as, lifted by volcanic heat,
   It meant to reach the sky,
Up ! up ! still up, until
The lowly vale became a lofty hill !
A-top of which
The Saint continued his sublime discourse,
With much augmented force ;
The solemn accents rolling full and rich
For miles and miles around.
The faithful could distinctly hear each sound ;
'Twas meet to celebrate
A miracle so great,
And so they built a church upon that hill,
Where it continues still.

Among the monks invited
St. Kined said he should have been delighted,
But age had made him weak,
   Crippled and crook'd
   His form until it look'd

Like a much damaged piece of the antique ;
   How could he come?   David his prayer outpour'd —
   Kined was *straight* restored
And walked upright and firmly on his feet,
Unto that saintly "meet."
But when anon he tried
Himself to do the like, it was denied.
St. Kined's prayer's went wrong,
His newly strengthen'd limbs no more were strong,
But doubled up again
To lameness and infirmity and pain.
Seeing all this,
The synod felt it would not be amiss
To have St. David for their Church's head.
Bishop Dabricius said,
   " My earthly sun is setting,
   Too old for work I'm getting,
So, Brother David, rule thou in my stead,"
And all the rest cried, " He's the man for us
To be Episcopus."
But David with humility refusing,
   Time and persuasion needed to be spent
   Before he would consent
To ratify their choosing.

   His fitness soon was proved ;
Deck'd with a Bishop's might and mitred crown,
   His station he removed
From Caerleon, the Tennysonian town
Of Arthur's great renown,

To settle in a district more sequester'd,
  Some wild monastic glen,
  " Far from the hum (and humbug too) of men."
  So, emigrating west'ard,
He chose Menevia, a secluded spot,
Tho' picturesque 'twas not,
Stony and barren, void of woods and rivers,
  In winter never warm,
  Exposed to ocean storm
And cutting winds that gave the monks the shivers,
But to such holy livers
It matter'd not what mundane ills they felt,
Or where on earth they dwelt.

Their rules were very strict ;
Speech was forbidden by an interdict,
And, saving when necessity compell'd,
His peace each brother held.
Dreadful to one who loves his tongue to wag
Must be such moral gag !
And then they had to work.
  " To labour is to pray," our Saint maintain'd,
  To *both* they were constrain'd,
Time was divided 'twixt the field and kirk,
'Twixt tilling earth and cultivating heaven.
Sins could not be forgiven
Until the erring one each secret thought
Had to his Abbot brought.
Strict, too, the stipulations for admission ;
Whatever his condition

Ten days the would-be friar had to wait
Outside the Abbey gate,
Bearing hard speech, refusal, irksome task,
And ask, and ask, and ask.
No entrance could he find,
Unless he left not hope but wealth behind.
Bread, roots, milk, water form'd the convent feasts ;
  David, tho' father and superior there,
  The same did share,
  He had no farther or superior fare :
And all the monks were clad in skins of beasts.

Not only as a priestly champion strong
Is David famed in song,
  A warrior, too, was he—on Badon's mount
The British army fought,
Routed the hosts the tyrant Saxons brought.
  To follow one account,
King Arthur—others say St. David—led it ;
  But all agree
  " It was a famous victory,"
Whosoever was the credit.
  'Twas then first worn,
  The fragrant leek did David's brow adorn ;
Thenceforward it became
As much a part of Cambria's name and fame
  As ours the Lion and the Unicorn.

Well, after a long while,
The holy man retired to Bardsey Isle,

And there the common fate
Smote him.   I don't exactly know the date—
Most writers say five-hundred-forty-four—
His age above four-score.
Among his other claims to be respected,
It should be recollected
That twelve Welsh monasteries he erected.

Alas, how Wales did mourn !
After his death the Saint was borne
To heaven in bliss to reign,
Right in the middle of a seraph train.
St. Kengitern—call'd Mungo by the Scotch—
That radiant scene did watch.
Oh, would that I had been by Mungo's side !
   (And now my words are serious, not jocular)
I surely would have spied
St. David's heavenward ride
   Thro' the clear medium of a strong " binocular."

St. David's legend—that is, history—closes
With that apotheosis,
A thousand miracles he wrought, 'tis said,
Long after he was dead,
And Glastonbury'd in that famous fane,
   Where Arthur's dust reposes ;
   But, not to be diffuse,
Our wit by brevity we must restrain,
   So, reader, please deduce
 The moral—plain as on your face your *nose* is.

St. David's name
In Celtic hearts high place must ever claim ;
And Cambria's ancient spirit is not dead,
For often may be read
Accounts of " Eisteddfodau"—festivals
Worthy the warlike halls
Of old Llewellyn.   Thither Wales invites
Her sons to see the rites
And hear the songs of Druid, Vate, and Bard,
Antique, but slightly marr'd
By newer customs clashing with the old:
Thus, we are told,
Each Druid wears his robe, and over that
A modern " stove-pipe " hat.
The " ancient Britons," too, of present date,   ·
On David's Day keep state,
And wear or eat the leek ; St. James's Hall
(St. David's for the time),
Responsive to the patriotic call,
Its patrons treats to Cambrian air and rhyme—
A very pleasant way
Of doing honour to St. David's Day ;
I, tho' of other race,
Can feel half Welsh when this is taking place ;
" The Men of Harlech" fires me,
" Poor Mary Ann " inspires me ;
I love to mark
The " Rising of the Sun," and " of the Lark,"
My bosom swells
On hearing Aberdovey's fairy " Bells ; "

I love " Llwyn On," and hang upon the tones
Of dulcet " Jenny Jones"—
Each brings a recollection
Of how, long since, I heard then to perfection
From native harp in sweet Llangollen's vale.
   (For wayward wandering was in youth my habit),
To me such melodies can ne'er grow stale ;
  I'd follow anywhere
  To hunt an old Welsh air,
Although I never could digest " Welsh rabbit.'

No. 13.—ST. PATRICK OF IRELAND.

Prelude—Harp Solo.

H ! blame not the bard, if he try all his powers
  To rival a minstrel so lofty in fame,
  Not born to match MOORE, yet in happier
  hours
His song may be touch'd by as genial a flame ;
The harp of Hibernia at present's his lyre,
  And 'tis of St. Patrick the tale he'll impart,
A theme that will warm, like a cheerful turf-fire,
  The cockles of ev'ry true *Pat*-riot's heart.

———————

In that delightful district of N.B.,
The first that (in its proper place) you'll see,
Where softly flows the Clyde (then call'd the *Cluith*),
There passed his happy childhood and his youth
The great St. Patrick.   In his lineage long
The "noble Roman" element was strong.
His father was Calphurnius, or Calpurn,
His mother's name Conchessa, as we learn,
Niece to the famed St. Martin, and no doubt
'Twas she who taught him first to be devout :
And so, for sixteen years he grew in grace,
When an unfortunate affair took place :—

Air—"Eveleen's Bower.

Oh ! weep for the hour
When, to steal and devour,
A band of heathen robbers to his father came,
Who sold his child to *them*,
An act we must condemn,
And relegate his memory to deathless shame ;
They took the captive child
To Erin's mountains wild,
And set him keeping porkers rather wild than tame,
In desert, glen, and wold,
Mid hunger, rain, and cold,
No wonder that he didn't much enjoy that same.

———————

One morn the swineherd o'er his fate
Was pondering disconsolate,
And as he listened to the wind
Thro' all his ragged garments blowing ;
And felt before, aside, behind,
The chill towards his marrow going—
He sigh'd to think how hard a case
It was to live in such a place.

" How happy ! " exclaim'd the youth so fair,
" Are the lucky mortals who dwell elsewhere !
Tho' hills be grand, and the pine-trees tall,
Tho' heather be gay and woodlands green,
And nice, *at a distance*, looks the scene,
One cheerful village is worth them all ;

O had I some snug little crib of my own
Far off from these deserts, so rugged and lc
With friends that I loved, and with money t
In peace and in comfort, what wouldn't I gi

Air—" Oft in the Stilly Night."

Oft in the chilly night,
  His guardian angels found him ;
One bade him quit by flight
    The woes that lay around him.
      Long was his trip
      To reach the ship,
And when he found it waiting,
    He fear'd to join,
    He had no coin,
A fact most aggravating.
    The rugged crew
    His value knew,
So back on board they bore him :
    Then off they sail'd,
    A storm prevail'd,
And sickly qualms came o'er him ;
  Next they were cast ashore
  Upon a howling waste,
Where for a month or more
  No mouthful did they taste,
    Until the Saint's
    Devout complaints

Had to the skies ascended ;
When lo ! a drove
Of swine arrove,
And so their famine ended.

Deserted youth ! how manifold
  His woes from slav'ry, want, and toil !
Once for a paltry *kettle* sold,
  Which, till his ransom, would not boil ;
Again, within his Scottish halls,
Our Saint received the angels' calls
  (They chose the night-time to appear in).
Voices he heard, from Ireland's shore,
His presence in that isle implore,
  Voices well worthy of his *Erin ;*
Yet duty calling, off he went,
And studied on the Continent,
  Improved his mind in France and Rome ;
And many a year abroad he stay'd
Until a bishop he was made,
  Then came as missionary home ;
'Twas thus the Pontiff Celestine
Invested him with powers divine :—

Air—" Come o'er the Sea."

" Go o'er the sea,
    Patrick, for me,
Strike at the heathens your stoutest blows ;

Erin hath need,
And the true creed
Gains the day wherever it goes."
So Patrick went over, the Irish delighting
With preaching and teaching, converting and writing.

Wouldn't my song
Grow over long
Should I one half of his deeds relate ?
Yes, I must touch
Only on such
As in his annals predominate,
Success and blessings his path surrounded,
Whilst pagan potentates he confounded.

Air.—" The Harp that Once."

The Saint has gone to Tara's halls
Mid Paynims fierce and dread,
The king to all his chieftains calls,
For vengeance on his head ;
When sudden, to their great amaze,
Eclipse the skies spreads o'er,
A dreadful earthquake rends and slays,
Till thousands are no more.

No more do heathen chiefs and knights
And other Tara " swells,"
Refuse to own baptismal rites,
No more their king rebels ;

To Christian truth each soul awakes,
St. P. his blessing gives,
Thus whilst his foes the Devil takes,
In honour still he lives.

Air—" The Woodpecker.'

'Twas shown by the cross that so gracefully gleam'd
O'er the path of the Saint, that a tombstone was near,
Yet he stopp'd not to pray, as a priest it beseem'd,
A fact which astonish'd his charioteer.

It was night when his saintship return'd to the ground,
Reminded the dead he should bless and bemoan,
All was silent around, and was heard not a sound
Save the holy man tapping the hollow tombstone.

" Oh !   Why did I miss such a duty ?" he cried,
" And who is the sinner that lies 'neath the mould?"
" I'm but a poor pagan," the dead one replied,
" So, of course, I've no right to the cross you behold ;

" By the shade of yon tree lies the Christian to whom
The cross appertains that is here by mistake,
Please take it and place it at once o'er his tomb,
For its weight is so great that it makes my bones ache."

'Twas done, the right grave by the emblem was deck'd,
Then off went the Saint in a satisfied mood.
So the Christian, now saved, went to heaven direct,
While the heathen, of course, had to go—where he could

Air—" Meeting of the Waters."

There's not in old Ireland an islet more sweet,
Than the isle where the penitents annually meet :
Oh ! the last spark of faith from the land must depart,
Ere pilgrims forbear on that journey to start.

It is not for Nature they go to the scene,
However romantic, sublime, or serene ;
'Tis not just for pleasure or holiday's sake,
They pay sixpence each to be row'd o'er the lake.

'Tis that Patrick the Great made a station for pray'r
With chapels and cells purgatorial there,
'Twas his own blessed crosier that hallowed the cave,
The heathen to slaughter, the faithful to save.

Sweet Isle of Lough Dearg ! by the devotees blest,
If ever I'm near thee, I'll go with the rest :
Oh ! may they in multitude yearly increase,
And the boatmen grow rich by their sixpence a-piece !

Air—" Let Erin remember."

Let Erin remember, in days of yore,
　　Before Saint Pat relieved her,
She swarm'd with reptiles and snakes galore,
　　And demons that greatly grieved her.

When Patrick scour'd the country round,
　　And hunted the venomous scourges,
He drove them up to a rocky ground,
　　That frown'd o'er the wild sea surges.

ST. PATRICK THE VERMIN-KILLER. "OH! SNAKES!"

The Saint then utter'd a holy spell,
  With his magic staff in motion,
Then over the creatures went pell-mell
  And perish'd within the ocean.

The devils he quell'd at a similar time,
  Tho' savagely they contested,
And never by vermin or fiendish crime
  Has Erin been since infested.

Air—'Tis believed of this Harp."

'Twas believed of our Saint that in miracles he
Surpass'd all the rest, of whatever degree,
That he once turn'd a wicked king into a fox,
And often caused fountains to spring from the rocks.

That he parted the waters like Moses of yore,
When missing the boat to the opposite shore ;
That whatever he curst or whomever he bless'd
Was blissfully lucky or deeply distress'd ;

That a poor little boy torn to pieces by swine,
Was join'd and revived by his power divine ;
That in childhood he once lit a fire with ice,
And cured a mad cow of demoniac vice.

That he turned snow to butter, and stones into cheese,
And anything else to whatever you please ;
That he caused a poor leper, whom no one would own,
To float o'er the waves on an altar of stone ;

That a lake and a palace some miles he removed,
To leave a retreat for a hermit he loved ;
And that, when at idols he pointed his staff,
They met with the fate of the Jews' golden calf ;

That once from St. Patrick was stolen a goat,
Kill'd, cook'd, and dispatch'd down the robber's own throat,
And when sev'ral men on suspicion were tried,
The goat bleated out from the culprit's inside !

That Eoghan, the ugliest chief of them all,
At Patrick's command turn'd both handsome and tall,
And that an old dotard he changed to a youth—
All this and far more was believed as the truth.

But should I one half of his miracles tell,
To epic dimensions this poem would swell ;
And had I the gifts of MOORE, LOVER, and PROUT,
My store to the sequel would scarcely hold out.

Let's run thro' the best, but in case you may tire,
I'll rest for awhile, and hand over my lyre
To one who of such information is full—
My friend Brian Dennis Macarthy O'Bull.

THE ACTS OF ST. PATRICK.

(MR. O'BULL'S VERSION.)

St. Patrick was the greatest Saint
    Of any age or nation,
And even what he *didn't* do
    Deserved canonization.

Whatever was impossible,
  St. Patrick could achieve it ;
I'll soon convince you all of this,
  Tho' you may ne'er believe it.

He cured the hungry, fed the lame,
  And gave the blind their hearing ;
To deaf and dumb he did the same,
  He was so persevering.

To be benevolent to all
  The Saint was always willing ;
He raised the *nearly* dead to life,
  His kindness was so " killing."

He cleansed the lepers—devils, too,
  Cast out with skill surprising ;
And on his birthday passed a week,
  Twelve thousand folks baptizing.

They gave him gold, but he refused,
  For dross he was not greedy ;
And even what he kept, he spent
  On those who were more needy.

And then the priests that he ordain'd,
  The convents that he founded—
So numerous were, that he himself
  When told, was quite astounded.

St. Patrick came to Erin by
  The Holy Pope's *mandamus ;*
No saint of such celebrity
  Was ever half so famous.

Once, forty days his nights he pass'd
　　In glory everlasting ;
His only fare or drink was pray'r,
　　But then he took it fasting.

'Twas there he saw our ransom'd souls
　　Like birds of brilliant feather ;
Some stopping as they pass'd him by,
　　Whilst all flew on together.

Whene'er he came across a cross,
　　He cross'd himself in token
Of rev'rence ; then stood kneeling while
　　His silent prayers were spoken.

But heathen gods and Druid stones,
　　He shunn'd with great persistence ;
Whenever he went near them, he
　　Would keep them at a distance.

The shamrock was his fav'rite flow'r,
　　In colour so excelling ;
Ah ! had it only a perfume,
　　'Twould beat the lot for smelling !

He did not introduce *poteen*,
　　As *has* been represented ;
For whisky was in Ireland known
　　Before it was invented.

St. Patrick's " Purgatory " stands
　　Of him a blest memorial ;
Where suffering pilgrims can enjoy
　　Their sorrows purgatorial.

His writings were so manifold, .
  That it has oft been stated,
Some books he was the author of
  By *others* were created.

For six-score years he lived, each day
  In goodness growing stronger ;
But had he died in recent times,
  He might have lived the longer]

His body's softly laid in *Down*,
  But time so steals and snatches,
No doubt the coffin's empty now,
  That holds his blessed ashes.

Saints Bridget, Patrick, and Columb—
  Stand second, first, and latest ;
Each one is equal to the rest,
  But Patrick is the greatest.

Then glory to St. Patrick's name,
  On fame's high summit set him ;
And may we keep his memory green,
  Long after we forget him.

Reader " I give thee all ; I can no more,"
("Tho' poor the off'ring be," perchance you add)
At least, if still you seek Patrician lore,
  Abundant books thereof are to be had ;
So I will finish what I have to say,
  In the light measure of a *Moore*-ish lay.

Air—" She is Far From the Land."

He is far from the land where his enemies·keep
  His worth and his virtues decrying,
In Britain his age will sink gently to sleep,
  ·The monks an asylum supplying ;

In Erin he lived, but in Somerset died,
  At (some say) a hundred-and-twenty,
Some less, but one fact all his records decide
  Of years and of honours he'd plenty.

" We'll lay him in state now," his followers said,
  " And send him to Erin to-morrow,
Where the shamrock will droop when it hears he is dead,
  And the blarney-stone soften with sorrow."

They gave him a grave in the city of Down,
  With other great saints they enshrined him ;
His wealth was but small, but his deathless renown
  Was worthy of leaving behind him.

Air—Love's Young Dream."

Oh ! the days are gone when saints so bright
    Amongst us throve,
And those who dealt in heaven's light
    A brisk trade drove ;
    New times have come,
    When Faith is numb,
  And all is gas and steam ;

Oh ! there's no one half so good in life
　　As our loved theme,
And nowadays how strange a life
　　Would Patrick's seem !

———

Farewell, farewell to thee, Ireland's protector,
　　Thy mem'ry I drink in a draught of " L.L."
If ever a " medium " shall show me thy spectre,
　　How gladly I'll bow to his mystical spell !

Farewell, farewell to fair Erin, thy daughter,
　　And may she grow ever more lovely and gay,
Forgetting the troubles the past may have brought her,
　　Till each shade of sorrow has vanished away.

　　　Air—" Dear Harp of my Country."

Dear Harp of Hibernia ! no longer I'll sound thee,
　　Already I fear I have jingled too long,
A wreath of absurdity weaving around thee,
　　Which serious people may censure as wrong.
Go, sleep till some rival of MOORE or of LOVER
　　Shall wake thy sweet strings to a worthier tone ;
I hope if I've hurt thee, thou soon wilt recover,
　　And mean, for the future, to leave thee alone.

O F relics and of holy charms, and such celestial treasures,
The Papal Church has ever had a goodly store to boast,
To priestly domination, of all soul-enslaving measures,
The traffic in such trinkets has contributed the most.

The " one original True Cross," as many Christians thought it,
Was cut, and chipped, and pared away to nothing, one would think ;
A piece was carried off by every devotee that sought it,
And yet from primal shape and size it never seemed to shrink.

Just so no monster gender'd in the mighty brain of Dante,
Had half as many bones and heads as saints, 'twould seem, possessed ;
And tho' of their identity the evidence was scanty,
In wearing such, believers thought themselves supremely blessed.

Yet how could any saint have had *two* sets of human members ?
And how could more than *one* True Cross as genuine be shown ?
Has any single year contained a couple of Decembers ?
Of *tongues* alone 'tis possible a multitude to own.

Besides, it's hard that Saints deceased, however much
  respected,
Are scatter'd in this fashion and not decently entomb'd,
Tho' calendar'd in memory, they're seldom *re-collected*,
But to a second martyrdom *posthumously* are doom'd.

Fair Italy in martyrs' blood's particularly wealthy,   .
  She keeps a bottle full in every monast'ry and church,
Which melts at prayer until it looks like fluid live and
  healthy,
  A miracle that well rewards the pious pilgrim's search.

Saints Ursula, Bartholomew, St. Vitus, and St. Lawrence,
  St. Eustace, John the Baptist, and some half a hundred
  more,
Have left their blood in Naples, Rome, and Sicily, and
  Florence,
  To liquify when holy men come thither to adore.

But 'mid the sacred relics for their virtues highly rated,
  St. Januarius's blood is famous far and near,
In May and in September is his *festa* celebrated,
  And once again repeated at the closing of the year.

Sweet Naples ! " City of the Waves," as Mrs. Hemans
  named thee,
  Oh, would I could do justice to thy beauty in my song,
And prove thee " Queen of Summer Seas," as poets have
  proclaim'd thee,
  But that would make the present lay inordinately long.

I

The subject of my melody's exclusively religious,
  I hope my treatment of it will be reverent to match ;
For one who ventures on a theme so sacred and prodigious,
  Should do his very best a strain devotional to catch.

Obliging Muse, come, gift me with an eloquence ecstatic,
  To praise St. Januarius for all that he has done.
(" Gennaro," his familiar name, sounds rather operatic,
  Suggesting dread " Lucrezia " and her vocalizing son.)

Would'st learn the Saint's biography ?—'tis little that is *told*
    of him,
  He preach'd at Benevento in the later Roman times,
When Diocletian's persecuting myrmidons got *hold* of him,
  Regarding his religion as the dreadfullest of crimes.

Of all the Christian prelates the position was precarious,
  When purple-mantled Anti-Christ the tyrant sceptre
    sway'd,
And thus it came to happen that the bishop Januarius
  To Pagan wrath and cruelty a sacrifice was made.

'Tis said it was Timotheus who, suffering from blindness,
  Was by our Saint restored to sight, yet doom'd him to his fate,
An instance that, as oft we find, to do a man a kindness,
  Is purchasing, not gratitute, but injury and hate.

The Saint was to the lions cast, to meet the fate of Daniel,
  With two companions, innocent of aught but holy zeal,
When lo ! each great *carnivorus* fawn'd on him like a
    spaniel,
  And lick'd his feet, declining to begin the horrid meal.

The lookers on attributed this miracle to magic,
   And charged St. J. with sorcery, whose punishment was
     death,
Determined that his exit should in any case be tragic,
   By amputation of his head they robb'd him of his breath.

'Tis strange, as I've remark'd before, that martyrs brought
   to slaughter,
   Whatever other forms of fate they manage to escape,
Tho' passing safe thro' boiling oil, and flames, and drowning
   water,
   Expire at once when death assumes decapitation's shape.

Tradition says, a Roman dame, his loss devoutly ruing,
   Sponged up the precious drops of blood, and put them in
     a phial ;
A bit of straw by chance fell in the bottle, while so doing,
   That straw's still there!—a fact enough to silence all
     denial.

The Saint's remains have often, since the day he went to
   heaven,
   Been moved from grave to grave, until at last they were
     transferr'd
To Naples' grand basilica, in fourteen-ninety-seven,
   And there with pomp and circumstance most solemnly in-
     terr'd.

The splendid tomb and chapel form a suitable memorial,
   Domenichino, Spagnoletto, were employed to paint
The scenes that deck the walls, and give a history pictorial
   Of all the deeds and labours of the wonder-working Saint.

It is behind the altar that the relics are deposited,
  And guarded safely with a double-duplicate of keys,
Till on the days of festival they're carefully uncloseted,
  The pious Neapolitans to edify and please.

The head of " San Gennaro," now as hard and brown as
    leather,
  Is placed upon the altar, near the sacrificial blood ;
The marvel is that when these holy relics meet together
  The vital stream will flow anew, tho' dried as thick as
    mud.

But first the guardians of the shrine, by fervency in praying,
  Must warm their zeal to melting pitch, to gain the need-
    ful power,
But when the blood will liquify exactly, there's no saying,
  It mostly takes ten minutes or a quarter of an hour.

A bust of Naples' patron, large, and hollow'd out, and
    burnish'd,
  Contains his fossil cranium, as it stands upon the shrine ;
With priestly robes magnificent his shoulders then are fur-
    nish'd,
  And when the candles are alight the sight is very fine.

The blood is kept in bottles, one is small and reddish yellow,
  But here and there upon the glass some sanguine specks
    have dried ;
The other phial's larger and more greyish than its fellow,
  And holds some half-a-pint or so of martyr'd blood inside.

The blood when first reveal'd to view is very dark and
    cloggy,
The case is like a carriage lamp, with hoops of silver
    barr'd,
The surface of the glassy sides is so opaque and foggy,
To *see through* the deception (if it *be* one) must be hard.

'Tis sweet to mark the faithful in the grand cathedral gather,
    To help the saints and clergy for their sins to intercede,
But if the blood's long melting, the officiating father
    Will try the soft persuasion of the Athanasian Creed.

That " fixes it," as Yankees say, as we should say, *un*-fixes ;
    The clotted gore is fluidized, and mingles in a stream
They lift the Roman candles up—the longest of " long
    sixes "
To cast upon the marvel their illuminating gleam.

Then when the process is complete, the keeper or
    " Thesaurer,"
    Like nursemaid with a baby, hands the precious burden
    round
To be caressed and fondly kiss'd by each devout adorer,
    With joyous tears, as one who has a priceless treasure
    found.

It certainly must be a scene religiously inspiring
    To see the pious multitude with pleasure so elate.
To hear the organ pealing, and the city guns a-firing,
    (But *that* was discontinued, it appears, in '68).

On special days the relics through the city streets are
carried,
A clerical procession as magnificent and bright
As monarch's when he's crown'd, or princely couples' when
they're married,
A "cynosure" all "neigh'bring eyes" to fasten and
delight.

When melts the blood a kerchief's waved, and birds are set
a-flying,
The priest upon the altar scatters petals of the rose,
And thus with praying, playing, paying (very often crying),
And marching round, the ceremony draws towards a
close.

No doubt 'tis most *imposing*, but suggestive, to my fancy,
(I hope that such comparison to no one seems a sin)
Of those ornate, bewildering displays of necromancy,
By conjurors like Hermann, Frikell, Maskelyne, and Lynn·

Oh, for the eye of childish faith, whose seeing is believing !
That faith which Education's spread is banishing from
earth,
Preventing lord or commoner such miracles receiving
As did in Jacobitish times the pious Earl of Perth.

The *festa* when he witness'd it took place in January,
Mid hundreds of the faithfullest of worshippers he knelt ;
He saw the liquefaction in the sacred reliquary,
And doubted not the Hand Divine had caused the blood
to melt.

'Twas only after many hours of penitential kneeling
  On cold, hard stones, the devotees beheld, with tears of
  bliss,
The blessed saint's death-frozen stream to fluid uncongeal-
  ing :
  The Scottish lord the bottle hugg'd with oft-repeated kiss.

Ah me ! this nineteenth century of scepticism and science,
  More cold and hard than any stones impress'd by pilgrim's
  knees,
Has taught that men, by bringing Nature's laws to due
  appliance,
  Objective miracles like this can imitate with ease.

,Tis hard to have to question such a sacred " Institution,"
  But Truth will stand, however close a scrutiny be made,
Applying to the mystery a chemical *solution*,
  We find there is no need at all for superhuman aid.

Thrice happy he whose calm belief declines the task of
  struggling
  With pros and cons, objections, doubts, all difficult to
  meet,
Suspecting holy ministrants of systematic juggling,
  And joining in a pious fraud the ignorant to cheat.

When once such possibilities have won from us admission,
  We find our doubts increasing while our faith is growing
  small,
Until their culmination in the terrible suspicion
  That Januarius's " blood " may not be blood at all.

And after all, *cui bono?* asks the soulless and prosaic,
　What benefit's the miracle, supposing it is true ?
Forbear, my gentle reader, whether clerical or laïc,
　To judge the creed of others from a narrow-minded view.

It keeps alive the ancient Faith which Italy, possessing,
　Is far more favour'd than ourselves, the godless tho' the
　　free,
A faith that thro' the centuries has ever proved a blessing
　(If this you doubt, peruse the Papal histories, and see).

Besides, when dread Vesuvius shows ugly signs of grumbling,
　The citizens implore their Saint the peril to avert,
And then, instead of lava-streams upon their houses
　tumbling,
　The fierce volcano stills its wrath, nor does the slightest
　　hurt.

For fourteen centuries or more the blood has now existed,
　For nearly half-a-thousand years its virtues have been
　proved ;
How many Roman converts in that time it has enlisted,
　How many souls from heresy to Orthodoxy moved !

Then hail to Januarius ! and may his feast tri-annual
　(Altho' they say it's scarcely so successful as of yore),
In spite of Garibaldi and Vittorio Emmanuel',
　In fame and might miraculous grow yearly more and
　more.

Teetotallers alone may well avoid it, since it teaches
Devotion to the *Bottle*, and it wouldn't do a bit
For apopletic subjects, for they know that, spite of leeches,
When once the *Blood* gets to the *Head*, they're sure to
have a fit.

No. 15.—St. CATHERINE of SIENNA.

" What does it all mean, Poet ? "

" Nor ever was, except i' the brains of men,
  More noise ! y word of mouth, than you hear now."

" Yonder's a fire ; into it goes my book,
  As who shall say me nay? and what the loss ?"—BROWNING.

LEND me thy lyre, "*O Robert, toi que j'aime.*"
Just for a little while, and, public, you
"Bid me discourse, I will *distract* thine ear"
With discords deep and grating to the teeth
As tearing linen, or slate pencil's scrape,
Or the harsh shriek of screech-owl on gnarled oak ;
Sounds jangled, tangled, like the knotted chords
Of Wagner's music-puzzlements ; vouchsafe,
O virile Muse ! to aid me to pour forth
Rhymes ragged, jagged as the rasping rush
Of rough Macadam emptied from a cart,
Or roaring cataract o'er rugged rock,
Lines like an iron tonic to the mind
Too smoothed by modern, milky, silky verse.
Make me abhor lucidity, and hide
My thoughts within a pyramid of words,
A verbal dust-heap, fleck'd with rags and bones,
Though priceless gems and gold will lurk beneath
So let my patient vot'ries grope and pore,
Read me ten times, and more, until at last
They think—poor fools !—they've found my meaning out.

1.

Where did I read St. Catherine's history?
At book-stall in the street of Holy-Well?
In dusty, fusty, musty bookworms' haunt?
In Record Office business-like and grim?
Not so, 'twas in a seaward cosy nook,
I' the vast library of the second floor
Of Count Montinfluenza's Palace damp,
At Venice, city of a hundred isles,
And twice a hundred kinds of colds and coughs,
Affections bronchial, and ague-fits;
For there is "water, water everywhere,"
Rising at a terrific (water-)rate:
That's where I found the book, all typograph'd
In middle-age Italian; I read and read
Until my heart, blood, body, brain, and soul,
Were full o' the subject, I must write or burst;
I choose to write, and this is the result.

II.

Hast ever seen Sienna?   No?
Then take a bard's advice, and go
When next at Italy you peep
Thro' Cook's Excursions (always cheap)
To see Art's treasures, heap on heap.
The City stands upon a jaggéd,
Scraggéd, up-draggéd, raggéd, craggéd
Cluster of rocks, where, long ago,
A fierce volcano boiled below;

Each now and then it mumbled, grumbled,
Rumbled, blew up, and houses tumbled,
Men stumbled, or in darkness fumbled,
Piazzas, streets, to fragments crumbled,
And in a vast *débris* lay jumbled ;
Thus standing on a former crater,
No streets could ever be unstraighter
Than those ; they are mere stairway cuttings
I' the steep rocks, whose massive juttings,
And green lapidical abuttings,
Are dented with these trenchant guttings.

III.

On the tip-top of the rocky perch
Stands Sienna's Cathedral Church,
Italo-Gothic, marble, painted,
Adorn'd with frescoes richly teinted,
Carving, mosaic, and in*laid* work
(Most beautiful and highly-*paid* work),
Walls, floor, and roof, in every part,
Are smother'd with results of art,
Tho' eye may see, and soul im*bibe* them,
Ruskin alone could well des*cribe* them,
Forget not, too, in that Ca*the*dral,
Some half-a-dozen of the *bead*-roll
Of Popish pontiffs, buried lying,
'Neath sculptures vast and edifying.

IV.

But Catherine ?—well, we'll come to *her*.
Up on the other peak or spur

O' the mountain, bleak, and bare, and dreary,
Rises St. Dominick's monastery,
A plain, brick building, heavy, ugly,
'Twixt the two points the city snugly
Lies in the gap; i' the midst doth stand a
Far-famous fountain—Fontebranda,
By Dante raised to Fame's high pinnacle.
A man of tastes and senses finical
Would hold his nose in going down
The street most noted in the town,
Full of the homes of dyers, skinners,
Folks of small wealth and scanty dinners,
Such poverty-polluted sinners
As one may see in Seven Dials
Or in the daily Bow-street trials.
The tourist shuns each *offal* sight
That wounds his feelings, left and right,
Yet, as the butterfly from worm,
In foulness glory finds its germ,
And 'twas from such a wretched place,
That blessed Catherine rose to grace ;
There is her house still shown, or rather
Old Benincasa's house (her father).
But we'll not linger there, her life
We have to trace ; the pruning knife
I'll try to wield for once, though never
In using it have I been clever ;
I leave to critics' great audacity
The task of stemming my loquacity.

V.

Well, but her life ? when born ? how nurst ?
Her starting was the very worst
For one who saintship sought of Heaven,
(Birth-year, one-three-and-nought-and-seven)
The youngest she of twenty-five
Children who did in course arrive
To Lapa her mamma (her sire
By occupation was a dyer),
And Catherine's kin were common folk
Held in this low world's grosser yoke.
Of course they fall'd to compre*hend* her,
And, tho' they thought their treatment tender,
To their own wishes tried to bend her,
And out of wits did almost send her,
Because they held conviction steady,
That she was out of them already.
For when they saw her take to fasting,
Weep, pray, and watch, for everlasting,
Indulging, too, in private flogging,
And every poor monk's footsteps dogging,
Mark'd her grow thinner than a hurdle,
And knew she wore an iron girdle,
And shirt of horsehair—her relations
With such proceedings had no patience,
They called it "fudge !" and made her drudge,
On errands trudge, thro' mud and sludge,
And yet, I judge, they owed no grudge
To her, who, lamb-like. bore it all,
Supported by her sacred " call."

VI.

For " call'd " she was, indeed ; at five
Years old, her faith was so alive
She, when she went upstairs, kept stopping,
And on her knees most humbly dropping,
Because she plainly saw up*on* a
Step just above, the blest Madonna,
Then, how she worshipp'd every friar
And priest, from novice up to prior.
In Dominick's monastery yonder !
Ev'n *presence* " made her heart grow fonder,"
Why, she would watch, with gaze devout,
Monks o' the abbey gate walk out ;
Then, when they'd pass, with sandal *shod*, on
She'd kiss the very stones they'd *trod* on !

VII.

Visions and ecstacies, you may be certain,
    Catherine had from her earliest youth,
Glimpses behind the mysterious curtain
    That shuts from our sight the pure essence of Truth ;
Heaven its glories unveil'd for her benefit,
    As for Ezekiel and John the Divine,
Ne'er a " trance medium," ghost-seeing, in *any* fit
    Bask'd in such splendours as she, I opine !
Saint and apostle would cluster and jostle
    Into her dreams, a celestial crowd ;
Each little cherub, like skylark or throstle,
    Sat singing sweet hymns on his favourite cloud ;

As she gazed, all amazed,
While the spacious heavens blazed,
Head upraised, lips that praised,
Senses raptured, chain'd, and dazed,
Still she gazed, gazed, gazed,
Till people very naturally thought she must be crazed.

VIII.

'Twas in her sixth year, when one day returning,
Her heart still fill'd with the holiest yearning,
Our little saintess beheld a sight
Of ecstacy, extra-heavenly bright.
She looked at the convent,—ah ! how she did love it !
But more at the skies that extended above it,
For there a light shone, the brightest e'er known,
I' the midst o' which was a golden throne,
And on it sat His form divine,
The Sacred Second of the Trine,
The robes of Popedom He had on,
Round him sat Peter, Paul, and John.

IX.

Each year her penances grew harder,
And more restricted was her larder,
At seven years old she would hardly eat,
Gave most of her food to the cats in the street,
Or else to her brother by way of a treat.
At thirteen years old she left off meat,
On getting to twenty, she gave up bread,
And ate raw vegetables instead.

And as for her food, good lack ! 'twas scantier still than her
    fare,
For fifteen minutes a day was all that fell to her share,
Thrice i' the day she flogg'd herself till blood ran down like
    rain,
And round her body, both day and night, she wore an iron
    chain.
And what, in one of her sex, is stranger still, she held
Her tongue for three whole years, by will alone compell'd,
Practice makes perfect in fasting, as in all else, it appears ;
And Catherine learned at last to go without food for years !

X.

The maidens of Italy marry
(Unless their plans miscarry)
From twelve years old to twenty,
When lovers, however plenty,
By ones and by driblets *drop* off,
For Southern charms soon *pop* off,
And Time sends each amorous *fop* off.
But Catherine of Sienna   .
Hated like salts and senna
All thoughts of men and marriage,
And beauty did much disparage,
For sure, 'tis a snare to many,
Besides, she hadn't any,
Or rather inclined to spoil it,
Than heighten it by the toilet ;
She look'd upon girlish vanity
As damning and deadly profanity.

K

Her married sister tried to make her
   Pay some regard to her appearance ;
Thus did the Saint awhile forsake her
   Strait path of heavenward perseverance ;
But scarce did such a change begin
When Catherine saw it was dreadful sin.
A Saint look smart, to steal the heart
Of Man in Matrimony's mart !
The bare thought pierced her like a dart ;
Even the priest would scarce persuade her
   To see that her sin was not so baleful ;
She, doubting if Heaven itself could aid her,
   Wept tears of penitence by the pailful.
The sister through whom our Saint thus swerved
Died early—a fate of course deserved.

XI.

Besides, wasn't Catherine married already ? you start,
But more you will start anon, when fully the truth I impart,
You know at the least, that a nun who the darker veil hath
      taken,
Is call'd " Bride of heaven "—a tie that never can be off-
      shaken ;
And Catherine's soul, from a babe on the cloister's life was
      centred,
It never could rest till those gates as a novice she had
      entered,
Tho' lying ill at the time, she pray'd them to accord her
The bliss of being a nun of Dominick's holy order.

Her mother and friends combined to carry her heart's
  petition,
And the convent sent a commission to test her for admis-
  sion.
'Twas one of the rules o'. the Order, at least in Sienna's
  city,
To shut the doors on candidates who happen'd to be pretty ;
And illness now upon Catherine had deeply left its traces
(It doesn't improve—not much—the finest and fairest faces),
All doubts were set at rest and distrustful feelings mollified,
For they own'd that, in *that* respect, at least, she was duly
  qualified ;
And so to her joy, the girl became a Dominican sister,
No doubt, despite her odd ways at home, her parents miss'd
  her ;
But family ties are as flax with children of Mother *Church*,
  friends,
They must leave their earthly mothers completely in the
  lurch, friends ;
And strong i' the faith, of her own free-will, our Saint didn't
  falter,
But sternly sever'd for ever all worldly bonds at the altar.
Fain would I dwell on her whole career, how, heavenward
  still aspiring,
Her fame and glory increased, but the reader might find it
  tiring,
It's lucky for him, perchance, I'm bound to a few brief pages,
Or I might run her history on in volumes, for ages and ages,
But all I have time to do is to touch upon points of pro-
  minence.

And show such facts as mark her religious and other pre-
dominence.

XII.

Miracles many our Saint achieved,
   Stranger than all the Saints before her ;
Ailments she cured, and pains relieved,
   Making her patients quite adore her ;
She seemed possessed of a strange facility,
In deeds of extra impossibility ;
Once she was giving some wine to the poor,
   Out of a barrel with scarcely a *drain* in it,
And using her might as a miracle-doer
   She caused it a barrel-full still to contain in it.
You've heard of those bottles which wizards are *skill'd* with
   Of seemingly magic, exhaustless interior ?
So Catherine's cask and the wine it seem'd *fill'd* with,
   To that first put in it was vastly superior ;
For she was in charity greatly abounding,
   And even would give what to others belongéd,
Her justification upon the plea grounding,
   That charity's right, whosoever is wrongéd.
She once gave a beggar a part of her raiment,
   He proved to be Heaven's great King in disguise,
And gave back the robe, which by way of repayment
   Was cover'd with gems of vast splendour and size.

XIII.

When Catherine's mother was stretch'd on the *bed* of death
   In mind and in body distracted and sore

The Saint interceded, and Lapa, in*stead* of death,
　Survived for half of a century more.
Once Catherine at the Sacrament,
　Rose in a visionary trance,
Her arms stretch'd out to full extent,
　(This is a fact and no romance)
Forming beyond all contradiction,
　The figure of the Crucifixion.
Forth from each hand and foot there came
A strange and dazzling ray of flame,
And from her sacred heart the same ;
A celestial illumination,
Amounting to Transfiguration.

XIV.

It grieves me, reader orthodox,
To give your reverent feelings shocks,
But saints of old could hob and nob,
　Familiar quite with heaven's denizens,
As with the meaner mundane mob ;
　Not only could they gain the benisons
Of seraph powers, and have each boon
Fulfilled both perfectly and soon.
To Catherine, renown allows
　'Mid all the sainted femininity,
The name and glory of the spouse
　Of the loved Son of the Divinity !
I know that I am on a theme
Which, in some eyes, profane must seem,
But *I* am not the culprit, *for* it is,
So written in the best au*tho*rities.

He wedded her with a ring of gold
  (Invisible to all but her),
And every time— so we are told—
  She sought her cell—so they aver—
There did appear, distinct and *nigh* a
Celestial form—the blest Messiah ;
And sometimes by his side another
Form—that of "his most glorious Mother."
He and his spiritual bride
Oft walked or glided side by side,
Pacing the lowly cell, by Him
Made glorious, erst so dim and grim,
Chanting the while some psalm or hymn
With chorus of the Cherubim.

XV.

You're right, intelligent peruser,
  To say such statements *sound* profane,
Doubting them, still you can't refuse her
  The credit of an active brain,
Which peopled vacancy with glories,
And caused the most astounding stories.
Either 'twas thus, or else, indeed,
  Such holy beings *did* accost her
To serve each heaven-aspiring need,
  Or else—she was a mere impostor.
Which was it ?   Let us try the question.
  You won't ?—you think your mind's digestion
Must fain be tax'd beyond its powers,
Should I keep on for hours and hours

ST. CATHERINE'S JOURNEY. "GOODS CAREFULLY REMOVED."

With psycho-theologic verse,
Such as MY mind loves to immerse
Itself in—diving out of sight :
You don't "feel like it ? "—p'r'aps you're right.

XVI.

Sackcloth and ashes, cowl and cope,
Catherine went to fetch the Pope ;
The faithful upon that mission sent her,
To bid his holiness Rome re-enter ;
The city, for lack of absent Gregory,
Was in a state of spiritual beggary.
Luggage of ladies, when they're travelling
Causes their cavaliers much cavilling,
Our Saint's effects were heavy and numb'rous,
And 'midst her *impedimenta* cumbrous
A portable altar she used to carry ;
Monk, priest, confessor, and secretary
Were in her train ; she'd a special "bull"
To give sinners absolution full.
The Pontiff, deaf on all other occasions,
Quickly gave in to the Saint's persuasions :
He left Avignon and went to *Rome* again,
Hola ! What pleasure to him safe *home* again!

XVII.

One day in a riot at Florence her piet-
-y made the insurgents subside and be quiet ;
    And did to its duty and reason the *city* call ;
Each rioter staightway slunk back thro' the gateway,
    Which shows the extent of her powers political.

Of Catherine's *works* some are left, but 'twere *irk*some
To give you long "quotes ; " each biographer *shirks*
  'em,
Some twenty-six prayers, and of letters four hundred,
Are there, and their style is a thing to be wonder'd
At, when we reflect that in reading and writing
She never took lessons, much more in inditing.
But heaven vouchsafed her direct inspiration,
Which surely's the grandest of all education.
If more you would learn of her story, go *to* a
Book written by " Raymond the Blest," of Cap*u*a,
A pious and diligent hagiographer,
Confessor to Catherine, and her biographer ;
Or if to her shrine you proceed on a visit,
Bow down to each relic, and rev'rently quiz it—
That scarcely is asking too much of you, *is* it?

XVIII.

In thirteen-hundred-and-eighty,
The saint we may nickname " Katey,"
Expired in Sanctity's odour,
And, whether by path, or broad *road*, or
Bye-way, or high door, or *low* door
Any door, some door, or *no* door,
That Heav'n she enter'd, to *sit* there
By virtue so perfectly *fit*, there
Can be not a spark of dubiety
To you, who have read of her piety.

Reader, farewell, if you have found, or find
A difficulty in getting out the pearls ·
From these, my rugged oyster-shells of rhyme,
Lament or curse your own stupidity,
Or want o' soul ; or slavish bowing-down
To the old laws of prosody and sense
Bards *once* obey'd ; dear Robert, thanks on thanks,
If I have hardly used thy muse aright,
If in recondite hintings I have fail'd,
Fall'n short in crabbèd verbal cragginess,
In ponderous elephantine march of phrase,
And paradoxical verbosity,—
If I have been too lucid—too inclined
To show, not hide, my thoughts—if 1 have miss'd
That sweet entanglement, delicious haze,
And fascinating fogginess, which lend
Thy works such charm, forgive me, I have *tried*,
Who does his best, great bard, can do no more.

No. 16.—THE VOYAGE OF ST. BRANDON.

THE land of Saints hath Erin been
From earliest early time,
Already Patrick's life you've seen
By me distill'd to rhyme ;

And now I sing St. Brandon's fame,
And soon you must concur
His travels make Munchausen tame,
And shame old Gulliver.

Till he was old he did not roam,
However much inclined,
Unless, while bodily at home,
He wander'd in his mind.

No paternoster-grinding friar,
Cell-prison'd all his days,
But Paradise, his chief desire,
He reach'd by other ways.

From good Barintus he had heard
Of blessèd isles afar,
Tho' modern maps say not a word
Of where or which they are.

The glories of that southern sphere.
So charm'd the good St. B.,
No more he'd stop at home to hear,
He'd rather go to *see*.

To sea he went, tho' whence, or what
   The tonnage of his bark,
His history explaineth not,
   But leaves us in the dark.

The Saint and twelve bold sailor-monks
   In *serge*—good wear for tars—
Exchanged their cells for fo'c's'le bunks,
   Their beads for ropes and spars.

But first they made a fast, no less
   Than forty days in length,
(The strangest way, I must confess,
   Of getting up their strength).

Yet fully was the vessel stored
   With food, and eke with drink ;
How long they'd have to live on board,
   Not one could even think.

'Twas thirteen hundred years ago,
   The compass was unknown,
To compass such a voyage, so
   Its boldness all must own.

Now, eastward ho ! their white sails fill,
   The breeze is fresh and fair,
And tho' " All's well," yet some are ill
   Awhile with *mal de mer*.

For forty days they sail'd, till land
　　Arose from out the main,
They thought it very lovely, and
　　They saw it very plain.

But tho' they tack'd, and turn'd, and back'd,
　　And cruised this isle about,
No creek, or bay, or other way
　　Therein could they make out.

A harbour at last! to shore they pass'd,
　　When down to the beach there came,
A dog of a breed I can't indeed
　　Quite specify by name.

He fawn'd at the feet of the good St. B.,
　　And bow'd and wow-wow'd with joy,
As much as to say, " I must let you see
　　How welcome you are, old boy ! "

To a hall well spread with drinks and meats
　　That canine led the way,
And beds were there with heavenly sheets,
　　And never a groat to pay.

And on the morrow, some shade of sorrow
　　They felt that place to leave,
While the " jolly dog " refused all prog,
　　To whine, and to moan, and grieve.

They sail'd and sail'd for a long, long time,
  All over the golden ocean,
But where they were, in what lines or clime,
  They hadn't the slightest notion.

At last they came to a bright green isle
  All dotted with snow-white fleece,
" The " Island of Sheep,"—they stay'd awhile
  In pastoral bliss and peace.

Each sheep was large as a full grown ox !
  " To you it must be clear,"
Said the hoary swain, who fed those flocks,
  " We've some fine *wether* here ! "

Ah me ! in these days of dear, dear meat,
  And frequent want and dearth,
When flesh to some is the rarest treat,
  What would'nt that isle be worth ?

" Oh, life is bliss in a place like this ! "
  Cried Brandon, " but tho' so nice,
We're off this week, for we have to seek
  The island of Paradise.

" 'Tis there, and not on this Isle of Sheep
  (Whatever our predilection)
Our Easter we'll pass, and so we'll keep
  In an *easterly* direction."

Anon our monks beheld an isle, that look'd
   Flat, dark, and barren as a reedy brake,
The brethren landed, and their dinner cook'd,
   When lo ! the ground beneath them 'gan to quake.
Frighten'd they fled : " You've made a grand mistake,"
   Exclaim'd our Saint, " from hence in haste we'll sail,
This is a *fish* that for an isle you take,
   That ever seeks in vain to put his tail
Into his monstrous mouth—'tis very like a whale."

Three days they sail'd again and found no land,
   Their hearts sank down in heavy doleful dumps,
The anger of the waves they had to stand,
   The rough, rude ocean gave them bumps and thumps,
And shipping seas compell'd them work the pumps ;
   At last they spied an island sweet and fair,
Where trees with spreading branches grew in clumps,
   Therefrom the notes of birdies fill'd the air—
So thick they swarm'd, the leaves were hidden where they
   were.

As on his knees St. Brandon, weeping, dropp'd,
The leading songster from his perch down hopp'd,
His pinions whistling " like a merry fyddle,"
And thus explain'd what must have seem'd a riddle—
" These birds were angels once, but Satan fell,
Dragging his seraph subjects down pell-mell,
To lowest depths, but some, whose guilt was less,
Stopped here half-way, to live in peacefulness,
Turn'd into birds, yet sing like angels still."

ST. BRANDON'S WHALING EXPEDITION.

Having explain'd, back hopp'd the bird to trill,
And with his mates the air with music fill ;
Singing as if it were "no song, no supper,"
And thus they warbled, in the style of Tupper,
Whose ode to our Princess is thought a fine
Sample of metre *Alexandra*-ine—
A poet arithmetical in fame,
Who "lisp'd in numbers, for the numbers came."

THE JOY BIRDS' ODE.

I.

100,000 welcomes ! *
100,000 welcomes ! !
And 100,000 more ! ! !
Oh ! happy birds of Eden,
Sing like the Star of Sweden,
Yes, yes, like Nilsson sing, birds,
And make the island ring, birds,
As no land rang before ;
And let the welkin roar,
To wel*kin* him to shore ;
Let miles of echo shout it,
And sparkling fountains spout it, {
Let leagues of lightning flash it,
And tons of thunder crash it ;
Let pouring rainfalls hail his name,
And fiery earthquakes sound his fame,
Till sky, and sea, and shore
Join in a vast *encore*,
100,000 welcomes,
And 100,000 more !

---

* To enable the reader to realise more vividly the impressive solemnity of this ode, the number of welcomes has been put in Arabic numerals.

II.

Oh ! happy, happy day !
Cheap, chip ! hip-hip—hooray !
Oh ! highly-favour'd land, on
Whose shore has come St. Brandon,
He comes, the Saint of Erin,
   A pearl ?—Oh, yes !—of price,
With twelve good monks of Erin,
To be as blessful *here*in
   As birds of Paradise.
He comes, the old and saintly man,
To do us all the good he can ;
Let crickets chirp his praises,
  And fireflies dance like blazes,
Let leaves in gladness flutter,
  And winds his virtues mutter,
Let Will-o'-the-Wisp his goodness lisp,
  And frogs glad croakings utter ;
Let sunbeams laugh and billows *roar*,
  And roll in gladness o'er and o'er,
Oh, let us all be *glad*, birds,
  And pipe away like *mad* birds,
His saintship to adore ;
And still this song outpour—
100,000,000 welcomes !
And 1,000,000,000 more !

St. B. and monks to bed retired,
  A night-long sleep to take,
The matin-song the sweet birds choir'd
  At morning bade them wake.

For—pious dickies !—every time
 Of prayer right well they knew,
At complins, vespers, matins, prime,
 They sang the service through !

When Trinity's great feast was past,
 Again the ship must ride
The billows of the ocean vast,
 Right on to Christmas-*tide*.

With tempests foul the wand'rers fought,
 And often pump'd and baled,
Until the land they long had sought,
 Those holy brothers hail'd.

" The Isle of Monks, oh ! blessed spot ! "
 St. Brandon cried, delighted,
" They'll welcome us, although we've not
 Been previously invited."

An old, old man (a monk, of course)
 Them to the abbey guided,
Whose brethren muster'd strong in force,
 And seem'd full well provided.

It surely was a wond'rous thing—
 A thing I can't explain—
What business those monks could bring,
 Out on that Southern main.

L

But so it was ;—"We all have come
From Ireland," quoth the prior,
" And on this isle we've found the sum
Of all we could desire.

" For eighty years, this Christmas-tide,
In gladness here we've dwelt,
And strange to say not one has died,
Nor any illness felt !

" We sow no corn, we feed no droves,
'Tis heaven provides our store,
Sending each day a dozen loaves,
On Sundays, twenty-four.

" And, since to guests it is not *meet*
To give an empty plate,
On this occasion, for a treat,
The loaves are forty-eight.

" So, Brother Brandon, sit you down,
No Christian can refuse
Bread made in heaven—both white and brown
Is there for you to choose."

Once Brandon there, as he knelt at prayer,
Beheld a form divine,
The angel who came—with a hand of flame,
To light the chapel shrine.

Twelve days, then off again, and thus
  From isle to isle our party
Sped on through perils numerous,
  And welcomes ever hearty.

Half the adventures that they met
  Were far too long to tell,
But some few specimens may yet
  Be pick'd from what befel.

With reefing and steering, and praying,
With tacking, mass-chanting, belaying,
  Their time was most gaily expended ;
Till a monster of aspect unpleasing,
  'Gan follow them, snorting and wheezing,
And clearly some mischief intended.

You've heard about sharks in the tropics,
And pork-baited hooks—for such topics,
  See Marryat, Cringle and others,—
Well, this, a still uglier " critter,"
Took aim at the vessel and hit her,
  In a way that astonish'd the brothers.

For into the hatches he spouted
Such torrents, the poor fellows doubted
  They'd five minutes longer to float ;
The vessel was rapidly sinking,
And small were their chances, I'm thinking,
  With never a life-buoy or boat

These creatures (their structures a puzzle,)
Have a blow-hole a-top of their muzzle
   (The *savans* have termed it a "spiracle ") ;
With this they their victims can worry,
But saints can't be kill'd in a hurry,
   There's always the chance of a miracle.

And so it turn'd out in the sequel,
The help to the need was quite equal,
   This monster, so bent upon slaughter,
Was quickly "chaw'd" up by a bigger,
Of far more Leviathan figure,
   Who follow'd him under the water ;

A peril now came, even harder,
Our monks look'd dismay'd at their larder.
   There scarce was sufficient to dine ;
They gave the poor steward a wigging.
When sudden they saw on the rigging,
   A bird with a branch of the vine.

Crowding sail on the ship, they soon brought her
To an island that made their mouths water ;
   For grapes grew as thick as wild berries ;
And there in safe harbour they glided,
For clearly the place was provided
   With natural ports—perhaps *sherries.*

The future our monks better beeding,
They victuall'd for forty days' feeding ;

Once more a new isle was in sight,
But it's folk made such gestures uncivil,
St. Brandon exclaim'd " Och ! the divil !"
And found with dismay he was right.

Eftsoons a fearsome sight was seen,
    That smote their heart with fear,
A sight that would have scared, I ween,
    The " Ancient Marinere."

A place, the name whereof I'll make
    To " ears polite " no mention,
Our doughty saint (he well might quake)
    Had reach'd without intention.

There grisly fiends, that gnash'd and hiss'd,
    And roaring sought the shore,
Hurl'd stones and darts, their aims were miss'd,
Or, sooth ! not saint nor crew, I wist
    Had ever departed more.

With yell and screech, each from the beach
    The holy men assail'd,
And nigh the ugsome Prince of Ill
    Had good St. Brandon "nail'd,"
But the heaven-sent breeze blew north'ard still,
    And still the vessel sail'd.

Escaped from these, they straight held mass,
    The monks their chorals hymning,
When shoals of herring, whiting, bass,
    Around the ship came swimming.

When mass was done, the pious fish
   'Gan peacefully disperse,
Anon there blew a breeze that grew
   Each moment worse and worse ;

St. Brandon steer'd, his men afear'd,
   Could nought but sink on knees ;
Some storm-fiend seem'd to haunt their ship,
And laugh as he held her in his grip—
   " I'll do as I jolly please ! "

Still on and on, anon, anon,
   Till the tossing bark grew stiller,
The tempest sank ; with many a thank
   St. Brandon left the tiller.

And o'er the main, now smooth again,
   The goodly vessel fleeted,
And came to a rock, whereon, in pain,
   A wretched wight was seated.

'Twas Judas of Iscariot,
   Sent up from the Blazing Pit,
And bound by a doom, in the storm and gloom,
   For days on the rock to sit.

His clothes were torn, and the waves had worn
   Off his " adipose deposit ; "
His ribs were bare as the fleshless sides
Of the grisly skeleton that hides
   (See proverb) in every closet.

" Alone, alone, all, all alone ! "
    Yet scarcely alone was he,
For a million, million fiends came there
    And they wouldn't let him be.

Good-sooth ! it was a gruesome sight
    To see 'em work him woe ;
Our saint compell'd with his holy might
    The demon crowd to go,
But they came again, in the saint's despite,
    And dragged their prey below.

St. Brandon turn'd with teary e'e,
    And left that place forlorn,
A sadder end a wiser saint
    He sail'd away that morn.

For seven long years St. Brandon roved,
    Ere he and his crew came home,
In Erin he lived, admired, beloved,
The rest of his days, till at ninety-four
He died, but he'll live on evermore,
    In the saintly roll of Rome.

And this is the tale of St. Brandon,
Its truth I don't venture to *stand* on
    And boldly defy contradiction ;
But if, upon trying, you find you
Can't swallow it, let me remind you
    That Truth may be stranger than Fiction.

Prelude.

WHO have sung, in verse not too sublime,
The saintly ones of old and modern time,
A subject which, unlike the poet's strength
And reader's patience, lasts to any length,
Take up once more my theme, my pen, my lyre,
Invoke the Muses for poetic fire,
Divine *afflatus*, and such other aids
As bards can borrow from the land of shades ;
An extra inspiration now I need,
A prancing Pegasus of purest breed,
For he whose life now comes within my scope,
Was not Saint only, he was also Pope.

His Early Life.

The story I'll relate
Of Gregory the Great,
Who every saintly quality possessed ;
And very soon, I ween,
You'll own he must have been
The best of the most blessèd of the blest.

In Rome he drew his birth
From a family of worth,
And Gordian of his father was the name ;
Who to a noble bride
By a *Gordian* knot was tied,
And Sylvia, it is stated, was the dame.

Both rich in Mammon's store,
But in piety much more,
In latter years these good patricians shrunk
From sinful worldly life,
And from senator and wife
They changed into a humble nun and monk.

'Tis always thought a boon
To be born with silver spoon
In mouth—and rather better if it's gold—
To Gregory this gift
Insured promotion swift—
Chief magistrate at thirty-four years old.

He lived in pomp and state
Befitting one so great,
In silk and gold and precious stones attired ;
But then his soul was set
On higher treasures yet,
To saintly reputation he aspired.

His Religious " Call."

No ! Gregory cared not for loaves or for fishes,
  Nor pleasures and honours that money could buy ;
The good of mankind was the aim of his wishes,
  And heaven the goal that attracted his eye.

And so, when of parents the Reaper bereft him,
  His personal cost was so strictly in bounds
That, from the magnificent fortune they left him,
  He lived on the pence and gave others the pounds.

He carried this Ruskin-like self-abnegation
  So far, all his titles and posts to resign,
To mortify pride and forego ostentation,
  Were serge 'stead of silk, and drink water for wine.

Six abbeys in lovely Sicilia he founded,
  A seventh—inscribed to St. Andrew—at Rome,
And soon, by his priests and disciples surrounded,
  As Abbot, Gregorius felt quite at home.

Ye Mysterye of ye Angel-Marinere.

  Now wonders began,
And heaven with manifestations impressed
  This sanctified man.
  Thus once he was keeping
  His vigil when, weeping,
And greatly distress'd,
  A sailor-like form,
Cast up by the storm,

Came thither to beg, and long woes to recount ;
  Much moved by his manner
  The saint gave a " tanner,"
(We look at the motive, and not the amount)
  And sent him away.
  But soon he came back, for his money was lost—
In grief and dismay ;—
  " Here's sixpence, my brother,
  Which makes, with the other,
A shilling you've cost."

  That coin went as well,
  And back to the cell
The sailor came—like a bad shilling himself.
  (What faith in his honour
  The reverend donor
Evinced, and how lavish of pity and pelf !)
  " I've no money left,"
The Abbot now said, " but this fine silver dish
  From begging and theft
  Will serve to secure you,
  When pawn'd 'twill insure you
Whatever you wish."

  The seaman once more
  Sought Gregory's door,
But changed to an angel's bright glorious state,
  " Hail, saint ! whose good action
  Gives such satisfaction,
I bring Heaven's blessing ; and here is your plate."

𝔅e 𝔖aint's 𝔉asting anb 𝔥umilitp.

'Twas said the good Gregorius was very fond of fasting,
But prone to faint with weakness if his abstinence were
　　lasting ;
For howsoever strong the will, and firm the resolution,
To realise their promptings oft depends on constitution.
He thought it very hard, indeed, that on the Eve of Easter,
When all the world were fasters, he alone should be a
　　feaster ;
But prayer and perseverance Nature's feebleness defeating,
In time he learnt to overcome that sinful knack of eating.
Beneath no bushel was concealed our hero's moral beacon,
For Gregory was nuncio, and cardinal and deacon,
Confounder of all heretics, and Papal secretary,
And sent to distant Angleland to act as missionary ;
But soon recalled— the Romans found they couldn't bear to
　　lose him.
Yet thanks for what he did for us no Briton can refuse
　　him ;
So great a "*pillar* of the Church," still high and higher
　　rising
Would reach the *Roman Capital* at last, beyond surmising ;
No *card-in-all* the Papal pack whose winning chance was
　　brighter,
No *lowly* head more certain of the *hier*archic mitre ;
Yea, once an angel told him so (the same he had befriended)
Who Gregory's "little dinners" in disguise had oft attended.
But 'gainst such high ambitious thoughts the humble saint
　　protested,

Declaring that his pious zeal was quite disinterested ;
"And if they offer'd him the crown" (and here the good
    man wept) "it
Would pass the power of all mankind to force him to accept
    it."
He little thought this attitude was just the course that won
    them :
Men always thrust their honours most on those who seek to
    shun them.

His Flight, Discovery, and Glorious Election.

But never were the Romans blind
To merits of the saintly kind,
They saw our hero was design'd
    For clerical regality,
So, when the good Pelagius went
Where popes all go when life is spent,
All meant to Gregory to present
    The honours of papality.

Now human nature, history proves,
In priestly bosoms lives and moves
As in more wordly forms and grooves,
    'Tis changed but in condition ;
The Church hath ever loved intrigue,
Each conclave is a clique or league,
Whose members work, without fatigue,
    The workings of ambition.

But Gregory, humble, selfless, pure,
Wish'd only to remain obscure,
And make his path to heaven secure.
　　He shunn'd both power and splendour,
And so in secret did depart
From Rome, conceal'd within a cart,
Resolving in his inmost heart,
　　He never would surrender.

Three days in caverns, and amid
The fastnesses of woods he hid,
He knew they'd seek him—and they did,
　　Most eager were their searches ;
They sought him north, south, west, and east,
By day and night they never ceased,
In Rome excitement still increased,
　　And tumult fill'd the churches.

Anxiety had reached its pitch,
They'd hunted every nook and niche,
At last they found him in a ditch
　　(I hope it was a dry one) ;
A sharp-eyed monk dispell'd despair
By sudden shouting, " I declare
The holy man's snugged up in there—
　　By Jingo ! he's a sly one ! "

But what secured his being found
Was that, as o'er some hallow'd ground,
A shaft of light shone all around,
　　Whose beams the ditch did *flash* on ;

And on the good saint's humble gown
And face, as 'twere some *halo*'d crown,
While angels flitted up and down,
   In Jacob's-ladder fashion.

'Twas clear from this that Heaven decreed
Gregorius to be Pope indeed ;
They fetched him forth with joy and speed,
   And hastened to proclaim him ;
So he was crown'd in pomp and state,
The Roman people, much elate,
Hail'd him as " Gregory the Great,"
   Which history still doth name him.

Blissfull State of ye Holy Father.

Oh ! what a glorious feeling it must be
   To sit enthroned in Peter's sacred chair—
To wear the tri-crown'd beehive, and to see
   Tokens of your dominion everywhere !
To hold the keys of New Jerusalem,
   And ope its radiant gates to the elect ;
Able to give salvation, or condemn,
   To breathe the incense sweet of man's respect.

To be a king, yet know no kingly cares,
   As royal quarrels, marriages, and dowers ;
Cousins who plot, or *too* expectant heirs,
   No queen to share (and p'rhaps usurp) your powers.

To know you are infallible, and speak
   Words prized as gems of wisdom far and wide !
No wonder human nature, being weak—
   (If popes *are* human)—should be puff'd with pride.
But he, our saint, whom nothing could make proud,
   Bore his thick honours, blushing all the while,
Adopting,—tho' so worshipp'd by the crowd,
   " Servus servorum Dei " as his style.
Some say 'twas nothing but " the pride which apes
   Humility ; " his virtues were a sham,
Pshaw !—slander is a thing that none escapes,
   Whom many bless, a few are sure to damn.

𝔐𝔞𝔯𝔟𝔢𝔩𝔩𝔬𝔲𝔰 ℜ𝔢𝔩𝔦𝔠𝔰 𝔬𝔣 𝔶𝔢 𝔖𝔞𝔦𝔫𝔱.

Of relics our saint had a number,
   And taught the elect how to prize
What sceptics consider as lumber,
   And heretics laugh at as lies ;
Miraculous legend and story
   He told, and much miracle wrought,
To Rome—be it said to his glory—
   The arm of St. Andrew he brought.
When sinners indulged in revilings
   The head of St. Luke awed them all ;
He'd also some precious steel filings
   Rasped off from the chains of St. Paul.
He sent to devout Constantina
   A veil the apostles had touch'd ;
Worth more than the oldest of china,
   By fancier eagerly clutch'd.

He'd oils from the tombs of the martyrs,
  That caused every ailment to fly,
And suppliants came from all quarters
  To ask, and he'd never deny ;
Such seekers his palace oft crowded ;
  When certain ambassadors came,
He gave them a cloth which had shrouded
  Some saints of exceptional fame.
The present afforded much pleasure,
  And homeward its casket they bore,
But found, when they peep'd at their treasure,
  A plain piece of linen—no more.
" His Holiness, sure, is deceiving,"
  They cried, and to Gregory sped,
Who then, to ensure their believing,
  Cut through the blest sheet—and it *bled!*

He Exorciseth Devils and Attracteth Angels.

Oh, doubt not such facts ; once St. Gregory, blessing
  A chapel polluted by Arianism,
Brought thither the relics he joy'd in possessing
  To aid in destroying that horrible schism ;
When out of the chapel a great hog ran grunting
  (Though how he got in there, I'm sure I can't say) ;
Of course 'twas the Devil disguised, who confronting
  Those sanctified symbols, was driven away.

The lamps of that temple by angels were *lit*, too,
  Or lighted, at least, when no mortal was near,
With flame so celestial in brightness, 'twas *fit* to
  Illume not an earthly, but heavenly sphere.

M

At times a bright cloud would descend on the altar,
The fane would be fill'd with an odour divine ;
The faithful that crowded the portals would falter,
Prevented by awe from approaching the shrine.

A Misbeliever Rebuked.

Sinners were many, in spite of saints,
Scorning the Church's high restraints ;
Doubting even the solemn fact
That Transubstantiation's act
Could change the nature of bread and wine ;
One woman, during that rite divine,
Presumed to laugh when Gregory said,
" This is flesh, though it looks like bread."
" What ! laughing at such a time and place ! "
" I'm the baker's wife, an' it please your Grace,
I made that bread, which is sweet and fresh,
But fain must laugh when you call it flesh."
Need I say that the Pope was bound
Such profanity to confound ?
Putting forth his marvellous power,
No longer the bread seem'd made of flour ;
'Twas palpable flesh, as all might see,
And raised their faith to the highest degree.
Hey ! presto ! again the charm he wrought,
And flesh became bread, as quick as thought.
All saw and believed, and the woman's doubt
Was changed to penitence most devout.

THREATENED OVERTHROW OF THE POPE.

His Charitye, Mercie, and Triumph ore ye Devyl.

In charity our Saint excell'd,
  Gave distant convents constant aid,
  Did many to the Faith persuade,
But none by violence compell'd ;
  To every sect was tolerance shown,
  And even the Jews he let alone.

Yet could he be severe at times :—
  A man the Church's wrath incurr'd,
  So Gregory spoke the fatal word
Which barr'd his way to heavenly climes ;
  The sinner, invoking magic force,
  Made Satan enter the Pontiff's horse.

As Gregory thro' the streets did ride
  His steed 'gan so insanely act,
  So plunged and caper'd, buck'd and back'd,
" The Devil's in him ! " Gregory cried ;
  The common folk, as he pranced along,
  Cried, " Here's another good horse gone wrong ! "

The Pontiff made the sacred sign,
  And pray'd a prayer ; the steed became
  At once as gentle and as tame
As any cat of yours or mine,
  Else surely, terrible to repeat,
  The thronèd Pope would have *lost his seat.*

Acts, Works, and Dethe of St. Gregorye.

'Twould take a most portentous tome
  To tell one half the actions
Done by the saint who ruled in Rome,
  His laws, his benefactions,
His doctrines, and his miracles—
  All more or less veracious;
Tho' some of those tradition tells
  Need faith both deep and spacious.
The church with ritual he surcharged
  (Already more than ample),
And her formalities enlarged
  By precept and example.
St. Gregory's writings, well 'tis known,
  Exist in great variety,
And tho' you may dislike their tone,
  You can't dispute their piety.
To prompt the work, the Sacred Dove,
  Upon his shoulder seated,
Would whisper faith, and hope, and love,
  Which he with pen repeated.
There was no doubt about the bird,
  For Deacon Peter saw it;
And died a martyr to his word,
  So *Fancy* did not draw it.
Translated to the See of Heaven,
  His right preferment gaining,
Our Saint was freed from earthly leaven,
  The fourteenth year of reigning.

He Establyscheth ye Gregorian Chaunte.

A musical glory to Gregory, too,
  All histories tally in granting ;
To him did the Church owe the striking and new
" Gregorian " method of chanting.
Two schools he established the capital near,
  Where good little souls he'd the cure of,
And any young lad with a musical ear
  A *sound* education was sure of.
The books and the instruments Gregory used—
  Including his rods for correction—
Are visible still ; nor are tourists refused
  The honour and bliss of inspection.

Ye Moral Lesson.

And now for the quotient that winds up our sum,
  It needeth no sage to explain it—
It is that, tho' often promotion may come
  To those who deserve to attain it,
By merit success cannot always be scored,
  Bad luck our deservings may smother ;
So strive to make virtue itself its reward,
  For fear it may meet with no other.

L. Cowan & Co., Strathmore Printing Works, Perth.